LAGOS_2060

LAGOS_2060

EXCITING SCI-FI STORIES FROM NIGERIA

Curated by:

AYODELE ARIGBABU

Afolabi Muheez Ashiru. Okey Egboluche.
Chiagozie Fred Nwonwu. Kofo Akib.
Ayodele Arigbabu. Adebola Rayo. Terh Agbedeh.
Temitayo Olofinlua.

LAGOS, NIGERIA.

LAGOS_2060

ISBN: 978-978-934-411-6

First published in Nigeria in 2013 by
 Design And Dream Arts Enterprises (DADA books)
3/5 Ogun Abewela Street, P.O. Box 130 Ipaja, Lagos, Nigeria.
City Office: 1st Floor, 95 Bode Thomas Street, Surulere, Lagos, Nigeria.
Tel: 234-01-7451990, 2348033000499
e-mail: books@dadaenterprises.net, dreamarts.designagency@gmail.com
www.dadabooks.com

Illustrations by Ibrahim Ganiyu / IC Studios
Cover Design / Book Design by Ayodele Arigbabu

This collection is dedicated to all who approach science fiction writing with the excitement it deserves.

May you get from it commensurate enjoyment.

CONTENTS

Dedication........**pg. v**

Contents.......**pg. vii**

Appreciation.....**pg. ix**

Prelude.........**pg. xi**

Conversation with Nnedi Okorafor......**pg. xv**

1. Amphibian Attack by Afolabi Muheez Ashiru...**pg. 2**

2. Animals on the Run by Okey Egboluche.....**pg. 42**

3. Annihilation by Chiagozie Fred Nwonwu......**pg. 72**

4. A Starlit Night by Kofo Akib...........**pg. 106**

5. Cold Fusion by Ayodele Arigbabu.........**pg. 138**

6. Coming Home by Rayo Falade.........**pg. 170**

7. Mango Republic by Terh Agbedeh ....**pg. 180**

8. Metal Feet by Temitayo Olofinlua...........**pg. 200**

The Authors.......**pg. 211**

* **LΛGOS_2060** *

APPRECIATION

The publishers wish to thank Amaka Igwe Studios / The Centre For Excellence in Film & Media Studies for accommodating the LAGOS_2060 project at inception and giving the workshop a conducive space to flourish. Many thanks to Amaka Igwe and Chris Ihidero for being great collaborators and dream sharers.

We thank every writer who has participated and contributed stories and other writers who have remained enthusiastic about the project since 2010, cheering us on. Thanks to Fred Nwonwu for the transcript of the conversation with Nnedi Okorafor, the constant prodding and the help with the editing. Thanks to Adebola Rayo who threw a tantrum about the editing and Temitayo Olofinlua who was gracious enough to put in the time to do some copy editing. Our thanks also go out to Steve Rossiter for his impressive blog post on the Cinema and Fiction blog....we never get tired of sharing it on Facebook.

We would particularly like to thank Nnedi Okorafor who joined in on the workshop via Skype, for being significantly encouraging, not just to this project, but to the entire enterprise of having strong Nigerian and African voices share science fiction and fantasy stories on the global scene, as exemplified in her work.

Lastly, we wish to thank each reader who joins us on this adventure, as you journey with us through each story....may the force be with you! ;o)

PRELUDE

Science fiction provides an amazing avenue for catharsis, especially in an environment that has suffered stagnation for such a long time. Science fiction unhinges the mind and allows the writer to imagine ordinarily 'unthinkable' scenarios. The political stagnation Nigeria suffers can be interpreted within the context of a creative writing process; the nation's development has been stifled by a lack of imagination. The country remains bogged down in the present, enslaved to its past and quite shy of the future. With science fiction, writers who dare the future, give courage to others.

Fiction from Nigeria has gained world-wide prominence over the past century; however, despite the contributions of Nigerians all over the world to the furtherance of science, we have made limited input to the science fiction oeuvre. The LAGOS_2060 project was initiated to help tip the scale a little bit. In 2010, eight writers responded to a call and participated in a workshop process conceived to commemorate Nigeria's golden jubilee and aimed at stimulating an interest in science fiction writing. The writers were of different creative persuasions and at different levels in the development of their craft, but courageous enough to attempt to tackle sci-fi. We asked ourselves, what will Lagos evolve into in the next fifty years, taking into consideration the mega-city's rich history and on-going urban renewal efforts by the state government? What will it be like to live in Lagos one hundred years after Nigeria gained independence from the British?

Why Lagos? Well, Lagos is the city of the future. The architect and urban theorist Rem Koolhas and his Harvard Project on the City team are credited with the discovery of an unfolding anomaly. After several helicopter rides, breathtaking aerial photographs, a couple of mind bending books and perhaps some yoga, the theorists postulated that all other cities are aspiring towards Lagos' self-correcting, chaos driven urbanization patterns. They had discovered a closely guarded secret known to only a select few. They had found out that Lagos is the centre of the universe.

Curiosity about Lagos knows no end. Lagos is one of the most exciting cities in the world. The future of Lagos is closely linked to the future of the world given the rapid rate of urbanization in Africa, the shift in the economic center from the west and the reality that globalization has become; so everyone should be interested in what becomes of this behemoth of an urban experiment.

There were lots of science fiction references out there, however, the fact that we were relatively starting from tabula rasa as Nigerian writers, meant that we could take whatever liberties we liked; because we were not bogged down by any existing models, we could very well create our own models for science fiction writing. Lagos lends itself to experimentation and improvisation; we drew from the chaotic freedom the city offers to the best of our abilities.

The anthology that grew out of the workshop is telling in the different versions of the future it foretells. In Lagos_2060 - an unusual scenario planning exercise achieved through the power and magic of a creative writing programme - there are climate change induced natural disasters actively plugged by doomsday preachers of the day, there are serious government institutions involved in first rate science and more often than not, these institutions tackle and solve the energy crisis to various degrees of success. There are wars and near wars as Lagos threatens to secede from the Nigerian state to have full control of its own economy. There are robots, amphibious speed trains, psychedelic drugs and highly trained security operatives with conflicts of interest, but more importantly, there are the ubiquitous Lagos people, whose industry and inventiveness seems largely unchanged, despite how much their city has travailed in the intervening half century.

The whole aim of the workshop we had in 2010 was to stimulate c r e a t i v e m i n d s t o e x c e e d themselves in fiction writing. However, that stimulation can still be useful in birthing the creation of more works in other media that easily lend themselves to science fiction, media such as film, comic books and computer games. These are possibilities we hoped to be able to explore in future.

The future is already here.

-Ayodele Arigbabu.
Lagos, Nigeria.

CONVERSATION WITH NNEDI OKORAFOR

*An excerpt from a taped conversation with Nnedi Okorafor via Skype during the LAGOS_2060 workshop in 2010.

Toni Kan: You sent me an excerpt of your new book, *Who fears Death*, which I published in *Sunday Sun*. When I read it, I discovered there was a shift from what you did in *Zahrah the Windseeker*. It was more African, more magic realistic. In Africa, we don't make very clear distinctions between what is real and what is magical. It just extends from one to the other, like a logical step—you just step off the threshold and you are in another world. For a westerner it might be different but for us it is an extension of who we are. With that in mind, one wonders for how long we would describe your writing as fantasy.

Nnedi: I have written realistic fiction before. I write memoirs, I write non-fiction, I've written all kinds. I don't just write Science fiction and fantasy...it actually depends on what I feel. When I mix folklore with science fiction, people don't know what to do with it. When my book came out in 2005, people were completely confused. They did not know whether to put it on this or that bookshelf. The fantasy and other tags you are hearing are from my publisher. My publisher felt we needed to call it something. Most of the things I write are off a whole bunch of things: science fiction, magical realism, fantasy. I tend to keep away from tags, but when they have to put it on a bookshelf to sell it, I let them call it what they want.

Terh Agbedeh: I read your profile and I can't begin to say how smitten I was. I find it impressive that you teach and you do a lot of other things. How do you handle distraction? Tony just mentioned that you have another book out, how are you able to churn out all these books? How do you handle distraction from the internet, work and other sources?

Nnedi: I was an athlete before I became a writer. From age nine I played tennis, ran track and field and I was very good at it. I think my discipline in writing comes from having been an athlete. It is something that requires a lot of discipline—when you are training, when you are practising or when you are performing, there is a level of control you need to have. I am a very disciplined writer, I will sit up at the same time every day and write. I always read what I am writing and stop at a place that is exciting so that I will want to continue. Besides discipline, it is also important to be organised. I do everything exactly on time. If you have a party and you say it is for six, I am always there at six. I am always early, everyone else may come late. I have a seven-year-old, I teach and I have all these stuff that I am writing and all the other stuff going on in my life. Yet, I am very capable of tuning things out when I have to.

Terh Agbedeh: What book are you working on right now?

Nnedi: I am working on my next young adult book. It is called *Akata Witch*. I am working on the early drafts now.

Terh Agbedeh: Did you say *Akata Witch*?

Nnedi: Yes (*laughter*).

Terh Agbedeh: I just wanted to get that straight (*laughter*).

Ayo Arigbabu: Those of us that participated in this workshop are trying our hands at science fiction with the hope that we can make an impact. What chances do we have of breaking in on the scene like you have?

Nnedi: I think the chances are huge, I think science fiction lovers are hungry for science fiction from the African perspective. People are waiting for it, they are watching closely. So that is why I was happy to hear about this project, because I don't want to be the only one writing the stuff. I have been waiting for this type of writing to come out of Africa, out of Nigeria. People are watching very closely now. So anything that comes out of Africa right now will be read with a very keen eye. So whatever you put out there has to be really good.

Paul: What drives your passion to write? What do you want to communicate?

Nnedi: I know that when I write, I am not writing with a specific message, so the message comes out on its own. When I am writing, the story comes first. I am a very subconscious writer. I am not really thinking about what I am writing, it just kind of flows out and when I look back at it I see other things, other plot elements and I think 'okay, I need to straighten this and that out. I can't really say I am writing for specific ideologies, but there are certain things I like to see. I like to see African characters; I like to see strong female characters; I like to explore issues of spirituality, but not in the way that most people would expect, because I have different ideas about spirituality. So there is no specific 'what I am writing for' kind of thing, the ideas come out from what I am writing.

Paul: I believe to write is not ordinary, you must spend time at it and you must have a focus. You said you write strongly about women, I believe for your book to be ground breaking, it must be something that challenges people. I think that in itself is a cause. You might not have defined it but it is there, a cause for people to follow... If someone holds you at gunpoint, will you fight to write?

Nnedi: Sure!

Paul: That means it is a passion, it is something you are meant to do. You are ready to die for it, so it is already a cause. As you are using that power, that tool, to break grounds, you are creating new worlds and new forms. If you are not writing, what are you doing?

Nnedi: Working out (*laughter*). If I am not writing, I am reading. Let me address the first part: the passion, the need to write. I want to say that it is not just about the passion or the need to write. If I wasn't writing or couldn't write, I would probably do something else—I would start drawing, if I couldn't draw, I would paint, if I couldn't paint, I would dance, if I couldn't dance, I would find some other art form to express what is inside me, because before I was a writer I was an athlete. When I couldn't do athletics anymore—and that is a whole different story—I started writing. So it is not just the writing. There are things I feel I need to express. If you ask me what these things are, I will have a hard time articulating it. I can't articulate it, that's why I write. So I guess you could say writing is a way for me to articulate my thoughts.

Fred: I read your book "Zahrah the Wind Seeker" and I came off with the feeling that the girl is tall, then when I saw your picture I saw you are tall, with long dada locks and all. How of much you is in that book? The second question is this: I write fantasy of a sort, stories from Africa's pre –colonial past, like 2000 years in the past. How much chance does that kind of writing have in the West? I know it does not have much chance here, because the general view is that you are trying to write like Achebe.

Nnedi: Let me answer the second question first. There is room for that, especially if you are focussed. And that is the kind of advice I want to give to the project participants in general. Focus on the character and not the technology or the magic and all that. Create strong characters, build the story around strong characters. That is something I want everyone to remember, but yes, there is definitely space for that kind of writing. African Science fiction and fantasy... there is so little of it here in the western market, so little—I am virtually the only one, so it's like nothing, like a big hole that needs to be filled. For the first question, I based her mainly around my older sister who is taller than me. My older sister is very tall. The hair—it is ironical—yes I have dreadlocks, but Zahrah's dreadlocks was not based on me. I was fascinated by the whole dada myth, absolutely fascinated by the idea of children being born like that, and that was what got me writing about it. I have written about some other dada characters before Zahrah, a whole bunch of them, so I am just fascinated by the whole idea.

LAGOS_2060

1.

AMPHIBIAN ATTACK

BY

AFOLABI MUHEEZ ASHIRU

February 19, 2060

GOVERNOR AZIZ BABAJIDE OF LAGOS was extremely pissed off. The dark skinned governor who stood at about five-feet-ten took off his reading glasses and stared out of his office window. The sky had a reddish tinge. 'God knows how hot it is out there,' he thought. Even though his office was air-conditioned, he knew the temperature was sweltering outside. His second year in office was turning out to be a complete nightmare. The reddish tinge from the sky seemed to reflect his mood, as did the temperature outside. Governor Babajide was readying for an emergency meeting with his commissioners and was expecting a briefing of events from the Commissioner for Environmental Affairs. There had been some mysterious deaths in the state and it had to do with the change in the environment. He silently cursed his predecessor ex-Governor Kola Afolabi. He paused for a moment and then cautioned himself. If not for Afolabi's mistake, he may never have become the governor.

In 2055, Governor Afolabi had announced that the state would continue his predecessor's plan to introduce nuclear power.

The state had its own independent power source, separate from that of the Federal Government. Even though the Lagos State Power Generating Company (LASPOGCO) had done well in providing power supply in the state, there was still a need to provide additional power for the twenty five million residents of the state. Babajide was in favour of solar energy. He and his environmental friendly cohorts had raged and rallied against the plan. They also claimed it was too risky citing the 1986 Chernobyl disaster and the 2011 events in Japan. The incumbent government had brushed their complaints aside saying it was a plot by the opposition to undermine the government and the good work it was trying to do for the state.

In 2056, the nuclear power plant was already running. There were power stations in Epe, Ojo and Ikorodu. Governor Afolabi was applauded. Babajide and his people were labeled enemies of progress. For the first time since 1960, every corner of Lagos was lit. Afolabi was the saviour of Lagos. He was destined to run for a second term in office. Nobody wanted to challenge him.

December 20, 2057 became an unforgettable date in the history of Lagos and Nigeria as well. As the state prepared for Christmas, an earth shattering bang was heard in the late hours of the day. The nuclear plant in Ikorodu exploded! Millions of lives were lost and the environment suffered immensely. The other nuclear plants were shut down and evacuated. The cause of the explosion was never determined. It was vaguely blamed on human error. The state and its government were in chaos.

By the end of 2058, it was obvious that Afolabi's days in office were numbered. The only person who didn't realise this was the Governor. Babajide was seen as a prophet whose predictions had come true. He was also seen as the one who could save the state from the calamity of the Afolabi years. His campaign vilified Afolabi's regime to the extent that people were ready to believe that Afolabi blew up the power plant himself.

AMPHIBIAN ATTACK

When the elections were held in 2059, Babajide had ninety two percent of the votes. At this time there were only two political parties. Afolabi had just about eight percent of the votes! It had never happened in Nigerian politics that an incumbent governor would be thrashed without mercy at the polls.

Apart from Afolabi's unpopular regime, another reason why Babajide won the election was because of the Bright Life Group of companies. Five individuals, four men and one woman owned the Bright Life Group. The company was founded in 2048. The company was at the forefront of scientific research in Africa and was well respected round the world. The company's main focus was medicine, pharmaceuticals and genetics but they also dealt in agricultural and engineering products. The company came to world attention when in 2053, they came out with drugs that could cure sickle cell and AIDS. The company was also on the verge of launching drugs that could eliminate cancer cells without damaging non-cancerous cells in the body. The multi-billion Naira Company backed Babajide's campaign and became major stakeholders in his government.

When Babajide became governor, his major task was rebuilding Lagos and cleansing the environment. He had done well in these areas. Major roads were reconstructed, the rail system and water transportation network was rebuilt and the state invested heavily in solar power. As was expected, the Bright Life Group carried out a lot of these projects. All these had been done in less than a year. Never had Lagos had a governor so dedicated and forward thinking like Bababjide. The only regime that came close, according to analysts was the Fashola led government that held sway five decades ago.

The governor was already fatigued from doing so much in such a short time. He was feeling very smug, and then this latest disaster struck. People had been dying after being attacked by some poisonous frogs. It was taking another dimension. It was fast becoming an epidemic and his government had to act. The governor had a feeling it had to do with the side effects of the nuclear explosion. They were barely coping with the heat caused by the after effects, now this!

There was a knock on the door. 'Yes,' said the governor. His personal assistant, a tall, dark man in his late thirties came in, wearing a well tailored and shiny suit.

'It's time sir, all the commissioners are waiting for you.'

As the Governor walked into the conference room, all the commissioners stood up. Without slowing down to greet, Babajide raised his hand in acknowledgement. He hurried to his seat. He was not a man who got carried away with protocol. He was the only one not wearing an *agbada*. The issue at hand was more pressing.

There were ten commissioners in the room. The Commissioner for Environmental Affairs, Dr. Williams, was the main focus of the meeting. He sat two seats from the governor.

'Commissioner, what do you have for us?'

The commissioner folded his *agbada* as he stood and cleared his throat.

'Please sit down and go straight to the point. Forget protocol.'

Dr. Williams nodded. He picked a remote control and tapped a few buttons. The whole room went dark. A ghost-like female figure walked in seemingly through the wall. The wall on the right side of the room was turned into a screen. As the female began speaking, images began appearing on the wall. The governor couldn't help but smile. Williams knew how to get to him. The image and voice of the hologram were like that of his eight-year-old daughter.

'Last month, there were some mysterious deaths at Onikan. Some swimmers were attacked by unknown creatures. There were bite marks all over their bodies. Autopsies revealed the presence of toxic chemicals found on some species of amphibians in South America and Australia.'

The pictures on the screen were not viewer-friendly. Eight badly mutilated bodies were shown. Bite marks were all over their bodies with some slimy pink and white mucus-like substance oozing from some of the victims. Chunks of flesh, skin and bone were dripping all over the floor.

'Two weeks later, five students were attacked at the beach. Three died, two are in critical condition.'

'More deaths have been recorded. Fifty eight people have been killed so far. It was not until last week that the attacker was identified.'

The picture of an unusually large frog appeared on the screen. It was about the size of a soccer ball, black, with pink and white spots all over its body. Its mouth was slightly open to reveal sharp teeth like that of a piranha.

The commissioner for health asked 'What specie of frogs is this?'

'We have no idea.' Replied the hologram. 'There has never been anything like this on record. These frogs have the ability to bite and chew. Their jaws are unusually strong. To make matters worse, they seem to be able to survive in poorly oxygenated water. They sometimes emit this highly toxic, mucus-like substance from those spots that make it difficult for victims to survive if the victims ingest the liquid or if it somehow gets into their bloodstream. They have been attacking other species in the water and killing them.'

Dr. Williams tapped his buttons again. The hologram walked out of the room and the lights came back on.

'We can advise people not to go near water-ways, swamps, pools and lakes. That can reduce the number of casualties,' said the commissioner for sports.

The commissioner for transport did not look pleased 'If we shut down the waterways, the rail and roads will be stretched to the limits!'

'Even if we shut the water ways, it might do very little to stop the attacks. Some of the attacks occurred inside houses. These frogs are able to squeeze into tubes way smaller than they are!' Said Dr. Williams.

Babajide was worried. They didn't even have any idea where the creature came from. 'Could the existence of this strange frog be tied to the after effects of the nuclear explosion? I have been made to understand that strange mutations can occur due to nuclear radiation.'

'Sir' continued Dr. Williams. 'Biologists tend to use the presence of amphibians as a sign for a healthy environment. However, the discovery of these frogs seem to counter that theory as we all know, our environment is in a very bad shape. Notwithstanding, we were investigating that possibility because we had not found any other alternative.'

'You said "were"?' asked the governor, 'why did you stop?'

'There was an explosion in our lab two days ago!'

The governor remembered. It was on the news. A number of scientists and researchers had lost their lives. Sweat dripped down his forehead. The situation was only getting worse.

'We currently have two dead specimens with us. Of all our remaining scientists, only one has a reasonable knowledge of genetics.'

'How good is this scientist?' asked the governor.

'She is one of the best in her field. I'm even surprised she hasn't moved to one of the private institutions.'

The governor sighed. He had to act fast. 'We will shut down the waterways. We will also send out warnings to all our citizens telling them to be vigilant. Meanwhile, the state university and other research institutes need to start working overtime. Commissioner, get your scientist to work fast. I will get my friends at Bright Life to assist.

Sunday, 21 February, 2060.

Meetings between the owners of Bright Life and the governor were conducted via video conferencing. They were held in secrecy. Special security agents occasionally checked and scanned the video conferencing devices. The device was a two-way communication screen. A special agent usually arrived via an airbug. The sight of the agent or his airbug appearing before meetings with the governor was a normal occurrence at the Bright Life penthouse. Shaped like a helicopter, the airbug bears neither propeller nor blades, and has a short tail with no auxiliary blades. Tinted, with bulletproof glass, it operates on high-tech solar powered batteries and is used only by the Police. Fast and noiseless, it could carry six adults and their weapons. It was used to patrol the skies of Lagos and was very helpful in combatting crime. In fact, the use of the airbug had drastically reduced crime.

In 2020, a special intelligence unit, the MT1 (Monitoring Team 1) had been formed to put an end to the corrupt practices of cops, military and para-military officials. MT1 was an elite group of specially trained and highly intelligent officers. The team had succeeded in sanitising the force. Their officers were highly respected in military and para-military circles. Even army Generals feared them. The fear of MT1, it was said, was the beginning of wisdom.

The head office of Bright Life was located at a sky scraper in Victoria Island. The penthouse was where secret meetings were held. It was all glass except for the ceiling. It was also sound and bullet proof. An airbug landed on the terrace of the penthouse. A glass door was opened by one of the five people in the room. The officer who flew the airbug wore a blue uniform with a helmet. An MT1 officer. They preferred to keep their identity secret. The officer saluted the man, who acknowledged with a nod. The officer checked the screen manually. He ran his hands all over the screen checking for anything that seemed out of place. He then produced a small instrument about the size of a pen and switched it on. At first glance, the instrument looked like a small torch but it was actually an ASD - anti-spying device. He ran the light all over the screen. If there were any spy devices nearby, the white light of the ASD would turn red. Moments later, he flew off with his airbug.

The man who opened the door, Mr. Ali Hamza, the main man amongst the five owners of the organization, was a pot-bellied man with a slightly bald head. The youngest was thirty five year old James Adeniran Bello. Bello was a young tall dark guy notorious for his womanising. He inherited ownership from his father who passed away years earlier. There were also the Chika brothers Okey and Ugo. Okey was the older of the two. They were light skinned, fit and of average height. The only woman on the team was Mrs. Mary Dipriye, a beautiful widow in her mid-forties. She had the reputation of being a ruthless cougar and was rumoured to be having an affair with James.

They settled down in their seats. The atmosphere was tense, serious, like a courtroom during a murder trial. They sat in a small semi-circle with Hamza at the head, opposite the forty inches screen. The screen came on and the governor appeared.

After exchanging pleasantries, the governor asked the group to help in identifying and eliminating the killer frogs. The group agreed to help but James warned the governor- 'Sir, this is a capital-intensive project. We will start right away but it's going to cost the government a lot.'

'How much are we talking about?'

'A couple of billions sir.' Replied Okey.

'Alright just do your best and make it very quick.'

'How quick?' Mary asked.

'As quick as having the results yesterday!'

'No problem sir.' Said Hamza. We will begin immediately.'

After switching the screen off, Hamza grinned at his people who all had huge smiles on their faces. 'It is as we hoped, more money for the company!'

Monday, February 22, 2060.

Even in the early hours of the day, the heat on the streets of Lagos was terrible- aftermath of the nuclear explosion. The skies were hardly ever blue these days. The colours ranged from grey, to pink and orange. The city was largely being reconstructed, a number of the old buildings had to be demolished and rebuilt. Some landmark skyscrapers had collapsed when the explosion took place.

Mr. Dele Ahmed woke up with a terrible headache, the after-effect of a hangover. He dragged himself up from bed. The whole room looked woozy and swam slowly into focus. He stepped on the empty bottle of gin he had been drinking from and cursed as he reached for the remote control.

On screen, the governor's press secretary was warning citizens to stay away from ponds, lakes, rivers and beaches. He watched with little interest. The number of those who had died was bound to spook people. These rumours about some mysterious frogs and all didn't bother him. He wasn't interested in swimming.

He was an MT1 official and his job was all about catching bad guys especially those in the force. He lay down on the bed and closed his eyes. He would need a shower and something to eat. The hunger was chewing his guts. All of a sudden, he heard a voice that made his temper rise. The billionaire playboy, James Bello. He cursed and put off the television.

He paced round his room. The room was untidy, with clothes strewn everywhere. He missed his family. His ex-wife had left him, taking along his two kids, fed up with his habitual absence. At that time, he was one of the officers working on the security panel for political figures in the state. When she confronted him, his answer was always the same: he had gone on some covert business that he couldn't talk about. She left him one day. He came back to his three-bedroom apartment on the middle floor of the new three storey flats at Iponri estate and found a note on his bed. She had left two days before. With his MT1 connections, he was able to locate her. She had moved to a man-made Island off the coast of Badagry beach called Agbon Island. He was surprised that she could afford a house in that area. She did not pick his calls and kept dropping voice messages for him instead, telling him she never wanted to be with him again.

Eight years of coming home to a hot meal had spoilt him. To live as a bachelor was no longer appealing. Overcome by loneliness, he had decided to visit his family. If she didn't want to see him, he could at least see his kids.

It was a Saturday morning, the numerous coconut and palm trees that lined the beachfront and the streets enhanced the scenic beauty of the island. Though the heat shimmered, the air flowing in from the sea was fresh. It was still difficult for him to comprehend how she could afford such a place with her earnings from the head office of the Bright Life group. He pulled over in front of her apartment. It was a small bungalow with a short driveway bordered with beautiful flowers.

He didn't know if he would be well received. He wiped sweat off his forehead and walked to the entrance.

Before he could knock, the door flew open and his two kids Seun, the older boy and his sister Shola ran to him and jumped in his arms. He embraced them and carried them inside. As he dropped them in the parlour, two adults came out of the bedroom. One was his wife wearing a sleeping gown and the other was James Bello! So she had decided to flirt with her boss! The only thing that kept him sane was the presence of his children. No wonder she could afford the house. He left without saying a word. His only promise was to his kids; he would see them in school from time to time.

Since then, he had been living recklessly. A month after, he got his leave.

As he walked towards the window, he restrained himself from opening the window blinds. He took a peak outside. The black car he had been seeing for the past two weeks was there. For someone in his line of work, vigilance was second nature, he was trained to be vigilant. Nobody in this building owned that vehicle. He had a bad feeling about the car and decided to keep an eye on it.

7.00 am Monday, February 22, 2060.

Tara Johnson stood in front of the mirror. She examined herself. For a thirty-one-year-old widow, she didn't look too bad. She had been ordered by the commissioner to report to the office as early as possible. Resumption time was eight so she could still get to the office by eight. It was not often that the commissioner got to his office that early. She didn't want to be late. She dabbed her face with powder, packed her hair in a bun, grabbed her handbag and burst out of the door.

She paused to glance at her neighbour's door. He was a tall

good-looking man who she had met for the first time last week. Her car had refused to start and Dele Ahmed helped her out. There was something comforting about his presence. He said he was a cop. She hated cops. However, there was something about him. She hurried to her car when she remembered that she had a 'date' with the commissioner. Her car a Lagwon X10 was made by an indigenous car manufacturing company. It looked like a big grey egg with shining rims. She fought back the tears as the car reminded her of her husband. He gave her the car as a birthday present a year earlier. Two days later, he died in a plane crash. With no kids, she was single and alone.

'Open,' she ordered the car. The door on the driver's side flapped open like a bird raising its wing.

'Good morning Tara, destination please?' the car's electronic voice asked.

'Office.'

'Fasten your seat belt please!'

Not that she had to be reminded. The seatbelt fastened itself. The car came with its inbuilt navigation system. She had keyed a number of locations into its memory. She let the car's auto-pilot with its automatic sensors take control. She didn't want to drive this morning. The car found its way to the express road and was off to Ikeja.

Unknown to her, a black bus with tinted windows tailed her from her home. Dele Ahmed who had been watching the black bus noticed this oddity. Why was a black bus following his neighbour?

The meeting with the commissioner had been brief and straight to the point. She had been instructed to find out everything about the frogs. Of all the state scientists in the genetics and evolutionary studies section, she was the only one alive. Others had been killed in the explosion. The commissioner promised to provide everything she needed to carry out the assigned task.

A government car had driven her to a research institute where some scholars from the Lagos State University, the University of Lagos as well as other private universities were present. A doctor was showing the scholars some videos of the frogs. The newly found frog was seen in a pond with five African bullfrogs. The African bullfrog is notorious for its voracious appetite. It has been known to feed on other frogs, birds, lizards as well as snakes. The new species of frog was making mincemeat of the bullfrogs. It devoured two of them easily and was at the point of swallowing the third. One of the bullfrogs which had earlier attacked the new frog was struggling as if gasping for air. It was spitting out a mucus-like substance.

'Ladies and gentlemen, this is what we are up against. Imagine this frog attacking humans en masse!'

8.00pm. Tuesday, February 22, 2060.

Dayo was waiting for the girl at the lagoon front in University of Lagos. He had spent the last two days trying to woo her. She had finally agreed to meet him there today. He had been fantasising about the girl for the past one week. Shade, was small, athletic, light-skinned and had the cutest and curviest behind he had ever seen. Her athleticism fuelled his fantasy. Thank God his prayers had been answered. He just finished chewing some peppermint. He didn't want any bad smells when they started kissing. He also had a tablet of HAIVICURE; the drug made by the Bright Life group for curing AIDS. Thank God for them, he was going to give it to her skin to skin. If she got pregnant, that was her business.

He started pacing towards the water as he grew impatient. Why was she wasting his time? He was planning to give her a good bang and she was wasting time. He noticed something bubbling in the water. He went close to investigate. Something jumped out of the water and bit him in the neck. He struggled to get it off. It held on fast. He tried to run and tripped on a stone. More of them came out of the water and attacked him. He thrashed around and screamed for help as he felt his skin burning. Poisonous toxins melted his skin and sharp teeth chewed on his flesh. When the perpetrators were through, they dove into the water and swam away.

11.00 am. Wednesday, February 23, 2060
Shile left her classroom to use the toilet. She was an eight-year-old who attended one of the highbrow primary schools at Lekki. As young as she was, she was very cautious about using any toilet outside her home. She wiped the toilet seat clean and dry with some tissue. When she was through with the cleaning, she saw a huge bubble burst on the surface of the water in the closet. That was strange! She kept staring into the water closet when she saw a huge black thing with pink and white spots squeezing out of the waste pipe. She slammed the seat cover and flushed.
She waited a few seconds before opening the closet. Six frogs attacked her.

*   *   *

Mr. John heard a scream coming from the toilet. He was teaching English in class. He knew Shile, the governor's daughter had gone to the toilet. He ran to the toilet and barged through the door. There was blood everywhere. The frogs had eaten off all of Shile's flesh. More than a hundred of them were jumping around. Before he could make a run for freedom, they pounced.

All television and radio stations were airing the news. The governor's daughter, a teacher and five pupils had been killed in a freak attack by the killer frogs. The frogs attacked in large numbers and disappeared. They had been noticed in Lagos but there were fears that they may have already spread to neighbouring states and countries. Benin Republic and Cameroun shut their borders. Quarantine officials were deployed. A state of emergency was declared.
The pressure was on the scientists to find a solution to the problem. The government team and the scientists from Bright Life were doing all they could. Divers were scouring the lagoons and waterside looking for live specimen of the frogs. A team of government divers met their death at Apapa. The frogs devoured them and disappeared. This disappearing act of the frogs was what

baffled everybody. They were more like ghosts than actual frogs. Religious houses called for night vigils, fasting and marathon prayers.

The group from Bright Life captured five live specimens. Two were given to the government officials to work on. Tara was studying the genetic makeup of the frogs. She concluded that their makeup looked artificial. When she told the head of the team Professor Dada that she suspected it was a man-made phenomenon, he was sceptical about her findings.

'Tara, it could be the nuclear explosion causing this strange mutation.'

'I'm not disputing that sir. What I'm saying is that there are elements of human intervention here. They have genes responsible for their aggressive behaviour which match those found in higher carnivorous mammals. How do we explain that?'

'Nuclear radiation plus freak evolution.'

It was obvious he wasn't going to accept. She submitted her report and left.

Other scientists were working on various methods of eliminating the frogs. There was no natural predator that could tolerate the poisons being emitted by the frogs. Snakes, crocodiles, fishes, birds of prey and even domestic dogs and cats around the swampy areas of Lagos were dying in large numbers. Scientists tried to avoid using chemicals that could affect the environment. After various failed attempts, few options were left to the scientists.

The scientists from Bright Life were doing better, they had developed a chemical that could be used to destroy the frogs but were still testing it to see how environmentally friendly it was. The whole country waited impatiently.

8.00 am. Thursday, February 24, 2060

After another night in town drinking, Dele woke up with a hangover. He had picked a girl in town and after a night of rough sex, he was tired and extremely hungry. The girl told him she was leaving. He couldn't even remember her name! Grunting, he gave her some money to pay for a taxi and promised to call her later in the day. After trying unsuccessfully to sleep off the hunger, Dele got up. He opened the fridge. It was empty except for a loaf of bread and a jar of jam. He began chewing the loaf without applying the jam. Gone were the days when he would wake up to something hot and tasty! Cold bread would do.

He remembered the bus outside. He went to the window, pried open a section of the blind and peeked through. It was still there. He had to know why the bus was always there. He knew everybody on his block. Only three people on his block owned cars. All the occupants of the block opposite his owned cars but nobody owned a black bus like this. The black bus was a Ford. He could not see the plate number so he decided to go downstairs and have a better look. He didn't want to be taken by surprise so he took his gun along. His gun was a Nigerian made automatic pistol with an in-built silencer and could hold thirty rounds. He wore a cap, t-shirt and a pair of jeans. His gun was strapped to his belt.

He walked past the bus noting the plate number. It was hard to tell if someone was inside because it was heavily tinted. He didn't want to use any electronic device to check because he didn't know what devices the inhabitants of the car had with them. He also wasn't sure if he was the one being watched so he hid at the entrance of the building closest to the car and threw a stone at it. If there was nobody in it and the car was parked innocently, the alarm would go off. There was no sound. The window of the passenger side came down and a man in dark glasses peered out. There were at least two people in the car.

*　　　　　*　　　　　*

2.00 pm. Thursday, February 24, 2060
Dele kept watching the bus. He was well trained in surveillance so sitting by the window watching a static vehicle for hours meant nothing to him. He had checked the plate number of the car on his IC15 - a hand held device used by intelligence officers to track people as well as to confirm the authenticity of fingerprints, phone

numbers, receipts, drivers licenses, plate numbers and anything that could be stored in their database. It was registered to the Bright Life group. And it had not been declared missing or stolen. Why would a vehicle owned by the company be lurking outside this building every day?

The doors of the bus opened. Two men stepped out, they both wore white t-shirts and jeans. One had on a pair of glasses while the other obscured his face with a cap. They both came towards the building. About five minutes after they came into the building, there was a power outage. They must have done this so that surveillance cameras in the building would not pick them. Dele readied himself for what was to come. With his gun in hand, he opened a small peephole in the middle of the door. It was sometimes necessary to operate manually and the peephole was his idea. He watched as the two men broke into Tara's apartment. One of them had a cooler with him. They spent a couple of minutes there and came out. His instincts stopped him from going after the men. Power was restored just before they got into their bus and drove off.

4.47 pm.

Tara was exhausted. The committee members still doubted her work. They said the technology for fusing genes from different species was hard to come by. Tara stood her ground. If they didn't want to agree with her, good luck to them. The autopilot was doing the driving. The only snag was that the car did not go as fast as she would have preferred. Once anything came too close, especially another vehicle, the car slowed to maintain the required distance between the object and the car.

As she was about to enter her flat, a hand held her back. It was Dele.

'Hi' she said, surprised.

'I think you should be cautious about getting into your apartment.'

'Why?'

'You had some visitors.'

'Who?'

'Can't say for sure but we will soon find out.'

She keyed in the password for her door on a soft touch screen hidden under the manual door handle. The manual handle was used in the rare event of power outage.

The apartment was dark. Dele went in first with his gun, after checking for any tell-tale signs in case they had booby-trapped the door with explosives. Tara switched on the lights with her home remote.

There were five frogs in the room. One of them leapt at Dele. There was a clicking sound as Dele fired. The silencer ensured there was no loud gunshot. The bullet struck the frog in the middle of its abdomen while it was in mid-air. The frog scattered into many parts as blood, limbs and entrails showered the living room. It was similar to bursting a sachet of water in mid-air. Tara screamed! Another frog tried to attack. It leapt from one side of the living towards the humans. Its leap was so high that its back was just a few inches from touching the ceiling. It was aiming for Dele's head. He saw it coming in an arc from above. The frog met the same fate as its compatriot. It was dispatched with a pin point shot which left it in several pieces.

Two more frogs leapt at them. Tara shielded her head with her handbag. The frog hit the bag with a heavy thump. In spite of her fear, she managed to get the biting frog off her bag by repeatedly hitting it on the floor. Once the frog was on the floor, she stamped on it. Her shoe heel was slightly pointed. There was a splashing sound as a colourful mix of pink, black, red and white splashed on the floor. Dele shot the other. The last one tried to flee. It jumped from one point of the living room to the other as Dele tried to shoot it. After three failed shots, Dele stopped. It suddenly occurred to Tara that it might be looking for a water source. They both watched as the frog tried to jump through a closed window. The urge to capture a live specimen overcame Tara. She ran to her kitchen and emerged with a huge basin. She grabbed her handbag and flung it at the panicking frog. The bag hit the mark and the frog was slightly disorientated. With all the speed and strength she could muster, she dove, covering

the frog with the basin. She sat on the basin and looked up. Dele was watching her with the kind of look an adult gives to a misbehaving toddler.

Her living room was scattered and colourful with slime, blood and bits of flesh all over the place.

*   *   *

Dele took her to his apartment and told her what he had seen. They still had the live frog with them. They wrapped it in a discarded mosquito net. It had struggled and struggled and struggled till it was exhausted. It stared at them with bulging eyes. There was something aggressive in its tired eyes. She wanted to take it back to the lab for further testing. Dele was not too keen on that.

'Besides, those men who followed you will soon find out that you are alive. I don't know how or what you are thinking but it's obvious someone wants you dead.' Dele wanted her to see things from his perspective. He was a cop and he couldn't imagine everything had happened by coincidence. Bright Life had something to do with this and he was going to get to the bottom of it.

Tara didn't want to admit it but she was scared. If what Dele was saying was true, she was in deep trouble. Why would anybody want her dead?

'Who would want to kill me?' She asked.

Dele scratched his head. That was a million naira question. The frog started struggling again as if to remind them that it was still there.

'Let's start from the beginning. We might find something we have been overlooking.'

Tara narrated how she had been asked by the commissioner to work on the frogs. She also told him of her findings. Dele listened attentively. Occasionally, he would be distracted by the struggling frog. He had the urge to shoot it but instinct told him not to. Besides, Tara would not let him. There were very few live specimens in human custody. As Tara narrated, he knew there was something he couldn't place. He could smell an answer but he just couldn't put a finger on it.

'The attacks on people, what do the frogs usually do after

attacking?' he asked.

'They usually disappear.'

'Is that the normal thing for frogs to do?'

'Am I supposed to know the answer to that?'

'Of course! You are the scientist!'

'The term scientist is very broad. I am a geneticist not an expert in amphibian behavioural patterns!' She replied. 'By the way,' she continued 'Even if I was an amphibian expert, why would I know what frogs do after killing people? Frogs don't usually kill people!'

Something just clicked in his mind. It would either make him look like a genius or a complete buffoon in Tara's eyes. Considering that she was an intelligent and beautiful scientist, he preferred the former.

'Excuse me.' He said as he left a puzzled looking Tara and went to his room. He searched his official MT1 kit bag and found what he was looking; a small tracking device. It was as tiny as a groundnut.

He showed it to Tara 'this is a tracking device. We are going to put it in the frog and let it go.'

'No!' shouted Tara, 'we are not releasing it. A live frog is extremely valuable for my work.'

'Look at it this way. The frogs usually disappear after an attack. They are not ghosts, there has to be somewhere they are going. If you recall, this one was trying hard to find an escape route in your apartment.'

'That's because you were trying to kill it!'

'Yes, I was trying to kill it but think about what I'm saying. If we find out where the frogs are coming from, we might be on to something!'

There was some sense in what he was saying. She reluctantly agreed to go along with his suggestion. The thought of releasing the frog and losing it forever was unacceptable. However, if they could find their base, they would get more than enough live specimens.

Getting the device into the frog was quite challenging. They didn't want to make physical contact with it because of its poison, so they donned thick rubber gloves. After all the battling with the frogs, there might be a hidden cut somewhere on their bodies. The frog tried to attack them every time it had the chance. Dele was losing his patience. Tara finally knocked it unconscious by carefully smacking it across the head with a metal serving spoon. She carefully inserted the device into the back of the frog's mouth with the hope that the frog would swallow it as soon as it regained consciousness. Moments later, the plan worked. They took the frog outside and released it into a canal.

Dele watched the screen of his IC15, tracking the frog. All of a sudden, the precariousness of their situation finally hit him. He was in his house with a marked woman who he had just rescued. He had to move her out of the building. However, that would be very risky. The only way to move around without being spotted was with an airbug. He had to get to the station to get one but he didn't want to leave Tara behind.

She was sitting beside the window looking dejected and lost. It was already dark outside. Had it not been for the situation they were in, the window blinds should have been drawn with the lights on. The streetlights filtered in through the open window playing funny tricks with her features. As Dele walked up to her, she looked inviting in spite of her unhappy state. She looked at him as he approached, her beautiful eyes staring. He felt something twitch somewhere between his chest and his stomach.

'I need to get to the station. Will you be okay alone?'

He didn't want to leave her alone but it had to be done. She seemed to sense his fears and replied.

'Don't worry; I guess I can take care of myself.'

Before leaving he gave her the only other weapon he could lay his hand on; a 2005 model pistol.

'Do you know how to shoot?' he asked.

'No... this thing looks like it belongs in a museum.'

Dele smiled. Despite the situation, her humour was still there. 'It belonged to my grandfather who was a police officer. He gave me as a present when I joined the force.'

He took her through the rudiments of shooting. As his hand covered hers when he was showing her how to hold the gun, he felt a slight vibration. She also felt it because his hand twitched. She got it right without firing any shots. He fitted a silencer on the gun and hoped she didn't have to use it.

'Does someone else have your house keys or entrance code?' he asked before departing.

'No.'

'What's your entrance code?'

'Use my name and flat number.'

'Okay, don't attempt to go in there. I'll be back as soon as possible. Please, do not go to your apartment for any reason.'

After making sure that his flat was locked and secure, he entered her apartment and dropped a small device which looked like a mobile phone.

*   *   *

When he got back to his apartment, he was impressed by the fact that Tara had the gun pointed at the door as he entered. They both climbed to the roof and got into the airbug he came back with. The IC15 was on. He gave it to her to watch as he flew the airbug. The frog had swum a long distance in a very short time. It had stopped very close to Agbon Island. The airbug began its journey towards the man-made island.

The two men came back to Tara's apartment. By now, the frogs should have done what was required of them. Their job was just to make sure things had gone as planned. They followed the regular protocol of shutting off the power supply to the building before going in. This time, they had their infra-red goggles on.

The fact that apartment was spattered with blood and bits of flesh did not bother them. The only thing that baffled them was that there was no trace of human remains. They noticed a light blinking on the floor. A small device that looked like a small phone was the source.

Unknown to them, they had triggered a sensor on the device. The way it worked was that once a human came within a two-meter radius, it took ten seconds for the device to come on. After coming on, it allowed another ten seconds for it to be switched off. The only way to switch it off was with its twin which was in Dele's airbug.

The two men watched as the light blinked. They didn't know what it was. One of them picked it up and read what showed on the screen. It read 'Dead Man Walking!' The next and last thing the men saw was a flash of light. They never heard the explosion!

∗   ∗   ∗

The airbug flew across the Lagos skyline. For the first time, Tara saw Lagos from the inside of an airbug. The airbug didn't travel too high so she could make out some of the buildings she was seeing. The National Theatre was still an impressive building. The light rail track that ran from Orile all the way to Badagry somehow managed to survive the nuclear explosion. Some parts of the state still had no power supply. It pained her that just a few years ago, the whole state was well lit. She had imagined what Lagos would have looked like from above. Even with the pockets of darkness here and there, the roads still looked good. The Orile/Badagry express road was lit like a Christmas tree, streetlights running on solar power lit the long road. A train traveled on the well-lit tracks in the middle of the expressway. As they flew over Mile 2 and Festac, she stared out of the airbug, enjoying the seeming serenity. She wished she was down there living her life and doing her job in peace. Who were these people that wanted her dead and why? Life had dealt her some rough deals but this wasn't what she wanted. She struggled hard to hold back the tears.

She wanted to think of something that would take her mind off her present predicament. Dele seemed to be that distraction. She watched as he maneuvered the airbug. To her, the controls looked like something from outer space. There was a kind of artistic beauty in the way he manipulated the controls. His concentration further enhanced his handsome features. His grip on the controls was firm. She had felt that grip when he showed her how to hold his ancient pistol. She wasn't sure what made her twitch at that time. Maybe it was his grip or the thought of shooting a gun. Since her husband died, she had avoided men. This one was arousing some curiosity in her.

'Can I ask you a personal question?' she said.

'Go ahead.'

'How come you live alone?'

Dele sighed. He had wanted to ask her the same question back in his apartment when she said nobody else had access to her apartment.

He told her all about his wife and their issues. She noticed the pain in his voice when he spoke. When he was through, he also asked her why she lived alone. She told him about her late husband. He listened attentively but did not take his eyes off the windshield of the airbug.

The thought occurred to them at the same time. They had been living in the same building without realising that the one person was just as lonely and in need of company as the other.

*   *   *

The IC15 showed that the frog had stopped at a building off the shores of Agbon Island. Agbon Island got its name from the large presence of coconut trees. The island was similar to Palm Island in Dubai. It was constructed in 2020 to further boost the tourism potential of the ancient town of Badagry. The island was the part of Lagos where the rich and famous lived because of its proximity to the beach. Celebrities and politicians from neighboring countries owned houses there. In Dele's opinion, it was the area for the rich and senseless who didn't have anything else to do with their money.

Dele hovered round the building for a while. It looked like a warehouse. He landed the airbug far from the building. He picked up the IC15 and requested information about the building. It belonged to the Bright Life Group. He watched the building for a while. A security man from the building approached the airbbug. Dele stepped out; the security man should know that only cops used the airbug.

'Good evening sir,' said the security man.

'Evening.'

'Sir we noticed you circled the area before landing, hope there's no problem?'

'No, just routine patrol. I landed to take some fresh air. You know with the heat these days, you people living on Agbon Island dey enjoy o.' Dele wanted to probe more but he wanted to be subtle about it. If they had noticed him flying around, then the building must be well guarded.

'Oga, no talk like that now, we just dey work here. The big men own everything. People like us can't afford to live here.'

'My friend, your ogas pay you well now! Is it not one of the big companies that own this building?'

'Oga mi, no mind Bright Life. Dem no dey pay better money.'

'That your company na correct company. You no need complain nao?'

'Officer, I'm just a security man. The money no dey reach me.'

'By the way what do your people do in this building?'

'We no know, but we know they do some experiments here and they keep some specimen here. We just dey do security, we no dey enter inside.'

'Na wa o!'

'Oga, let me be on my way before my supervisor comes looking. Enjoy the fresh air.'

With that the security man left. Dele hopped into the airbug. As they left the island, he explained the information he had gathered to Tara. He had established that the building was heavily guarded and that it was used as a storage facility.

'It all adds up. At every stage, there is always the presence of something or someone from Bright Life. From the men watching your apartment, to the group assisting the state in finding an end to the problem, I can bet that this is where the frogs set out from, to attack people.'

'I find that hard to believe,' said Tara. 'What do they hope to achieve by doing this? They are at the forefront of science and technology in Africa. Why do something so unethical?'

'I have no idea. Since we can't walk up to their doorstep and ask, we have to find a way of putting a stop to it.'

'Do you think there is anything they can gain financially from all these?' she asked.

It was Dele's turn to reflect. 'It is possible. Even though they have gained so much, there may be more for them to gain. If they can successfully eradicate these frogs, the government will pay them for it. Where the government is unable to pay, they will give them a tax cut, so it's a win-win situation for them.'

They flew in silence. Tara understood why they wanted her out of the way. She had been the one who came to the conclusion that the frogs were genetically engineered. All those who might have detected it had all perished in the explosion. Now that she thought of it, the explosion might have been orchestrated by people from Bright Life. Were they so desperate to make profits at the expense of human lives? How many more people had to die to ensure that the company made more money?

While she was deep in thought, Dele brought the airbug down. They were already back in Iponri estate. As they approached their block, they noticed that there was a crowd.

'Wait here!' barked Dele as he hopped out of the airbug. He returned about five minutes later. 'There was an explosion in your apartment! Two bodies were found. They are yet to be identified but the assumption is that one of them is you!'

Tara covered her mouth with her hands. She was shocked. 'There's nothing to worry about,' continued Dele 'I set the explosion up. I figured our friends would return.'

Tears trickled down Tara's face. Dele hugged her and tried to console her. She didn't cry out, she just shed tears.

After a while, she looked up at Dele 'You know you are in debt. Don't you?'

'I don't understand.'

'When this is over, you are going to have to buy me a new set of household appliances!'

They both smiled as he hugged her again.

*   *   *

Dele and Tara slept in an inconspicuous hotel in Yaba. Dele wanted to ensure Tara's safety. There was no information about Tara on the news so he assumed that the bodies had not yet been identified. He wanted them to work quickly. They tried to develop a plan to destroy the frogs. They knew where the frogs were based. Tara would have preferred to go inside to take a look but that would be impossible. Dele wanted to use his police connections to force a search but Tara cautioned him.

'We have no idea what part of the building they keep the frogs. Even if you get a warrant to search the place, you might not find anything suspicious. Besides, a company as powerful as Bright Life which has been helpful to the government will not be so easy to fight.'

Dele thought about what she said. He picked up his IC15 and checked the location of the frog. It was at a company office in Apapa. He wouldn't be surprised if he put on the TV and there was news that the frog and its goons were chomping on people in that area.

'I need to find a way to set some explosives inside the base,' said Dele 'to blow those bastards to pieces!'

'If we do it your way, do you know how many innocent people will be killed? We can start with your friend, the security guy.'

'You know what they say about omelettes; can't make them without breaking a few eggs!'

'Then you won't be different from the people who artificially create frogs to kill people all in the name of making money.'

'I'm different; I just want to put a stop to the mess they created.'

'You seem to like blowing everything. Even my apartment was not immune to your fetish. There has to be a better way instead of blowing everything up.'

He knew what he was being accused of, but nothing would feel better than blowing the warehouse and all the offices of Bright Life. To add to the satisfaction he would gain from this, he would probably blow up James Bello too.

'Can I have your phone? I have no ideas where mine is,' asked Tara.

'I don't think you should be making calls now.'

'I don't want to make calls. I need to search for something on the internet.'

He gave her the phone without further questions. She began making inputs on the phone. All he could think about was blowing up the ware-house.

After some minutes of searching, she returned the phone. He watched with curiosity. She looked very smug.

'So, what was all that about?' he asked.

'I think I might have found an alternative solution to our problem but it is quite risky.'

'Let me hear it.'

'In 2025, scientists discovered that poisonous reptiles and amphibians were being killed by their own poison.'

'What?'

'Yes, you heard me; their own poison was killing them. In parts of Africa and South America, some of these species were dying in large numbers. When necropsies were carried out, it was discovered that a virus popularly called the 'Poison Virus' was responsible for this. The virus attacked the poison glands of these animals leaving the glands weak and unable to store poisons the animals used in hunting and defence. When the glands became weak, the poisons leaked into the internal system of these animals.

The more poisonous an animal was, the faster it died. The virus was also contagious and had almost rendered some species of snakes, like the black mamba, almost extinct. The virus could spread in water and air. Once the body fluids of these animals come in contact with the bodily fluid of infected animals from the same species, they became infected. For human beings, the virus wasn't so deadly. It caused sterility. After a lot of quarantine efforts, the virus was eradicated in 2045.'

'How does the virus help solve our problem?'

'I thought intelligence officers are supposed to be 'intelligent'! What I wanted to do was catch one of these frogs and inject it with the virus. It would infect the others once it gets back to their base and the whole population would be wiped out.'

This sounded like music to Dele's ears. If they used this method, they would destroy the frogs without raising suspicion. The next challenge was catching a live specimen.

'But you said the virus was eradicated,' Asked Dele, 'How are we supposed to get samples of the virus?'

'As a scientist with the State Ministry of Environmental Affairs, I have access to the classified laboratories.'

'What are those?'

'Classified labs are labs where researches that relate to threats to the population and environment are carried out. Samples of extinct and deadly disease-causing organisms are kept there strictly for research purposes. But since I am in hiding, it would be foolhardy for me to show up at the lab.'

'I can go and get it, can't I?'

'They won't allow you in. You have to be fully authorised to get in. And don't think of bombing your way in there because it is a government owned building. At different entrances, eye scans, finger prints and voice recognition machines are used to grant access. If your details aren't on the database, you can't get in. Only a classified group of researchers can go in.'

'The only way you can go in is with the permission from the Governor.'

Dele was pissed. As an officer of the law, he should have the right to go in there. So he had to get permission from the Governor! Anyway that shouldn't be difficult. The governor's chief security officer was a friend and senior colleague.

*　　　*　　　*

The Chief Security Officer (CSO) to the governor Mr. Dayo Ojeyemi was in his office. Ordinarily, he should have been with the governor on a trip to Kano State but the governor was mourning. The death of his daughter hit him hard. He felt sorry for the governor. Shile had been a cute girl who had an affinity for cleanliness. Everybody loved the child. To have died like that at an early age was devastating. He was staring at the governor's family picture when Dele knocked and entered his office. The two were familiar with each other. Dele saluted him and sat down without being told to. He wanted to joke about insubordination in the force, if a junior officer should walk into a senior officer's office and sit without being asked to when he noticed Dele's appearance. Dele looked a bit rough like someone who hadn't slept well.

'I heard you commandeered an airbug for some days.' He said.

'Sir, I will explain to you in due time but I need a favour from you. I want to have a one-on-one talk with the governor.'

'He is not in the mood for chit-chat. You heard what happened to his daughter.'

'What I have to say is closely related to that but it is very delicate. I need to get permission from him to obtain samples of a virus from the government classified laboratories.'

Ojeyemi looked at Dele as if he was wearing his boxers on his head.

'What in God's name are you trying to do with virus samples. You wouldn't even recognise a virus if it was in front of you!'

'Sir, it is a complex issue which I will explain to you when the time is right.'

Ojeyemi studied Dele. He didn't look like someone who had

started taking drugs. Apart from his occasional drinking, he was not aware that Dele had any other vices. They had worked together so he trusted him. Not having too much of a choice, he agreed to assist Dele. As the CSO to the governor, he had the power to get the permission for Dele without seeing the governor.

*   *   *

The governor was sitting alone in front of the television screen. He was absent-mindedly flicking through channels. The screen covered one of the walls in the living room. Shile's death had sapped every ounce of energy in his body. He had a clear picture of what she would have looked like in twenty years. He had fantasised about her graduation from the university, and how she would have looked on her wedding day. He had imagined himself giving his baby's hand to an eager young man on their wedding day! Instead, it had all turned out a parent's worst nightmare; burying his child's remains. Tears flowed down his face.

The television was on a religious station. A pastor was raving and ranting about the mysterious deaths in Lagos being a sign of the end times. He urged listeners to repent because the much talked about apocalypse was at hand! The governor was about to change the station when his phone rang. The man in charge of the classified laboratory called him to inform him that his CSO had authorised someone to pick up samples of a virus. The governor said there was no problem. After hanging up, he summoned the CSO to have him explain what had happened.

*   *   *

Dele landed the airbug in front of the governor's residence. He had barely collected the samples from the lab when Ojeyemi called him and told him the governor wanted to see them. Since he didn't know the real reason Dele needed the virus, he felt it would be better if Dele was present to explain to him. Dele agreed. Once Ojeyemi entered the airbug, he recognised Tara as the woman whose apartment was said to have caught fire on the news. He was shocked because the information being circulated was that her body had not yet been identified. Dele urged him to be patient. The sample of the virus was in a small, sealed container. It was in transparent liquid form. Tara stared at it, in thought for a moment, then pulled out a syringe from her handbag and drained the container of its content.

' Is that it?' Ojeyemi asked, eying the container with suspicion. He didn't know what kind of virus it was and he didn't want it anywhere near his person. Tara nodded. She then placed it in a rubber pouch before putting it in her purse.

Once they got out of the airbug, Tara felt relieved. She had been in the Airbug all day and the cramped space was becoming nauseating. The guards let them in. The governor was waiting in the living room. Tara couldn't believe the man looking deflated in a pair of black trousers and t-shirt was the governor. Ojeyemi quickly got Dele to tell the governor everything. Ojeyemi himself was as shocked as the governor when he heard the whole story. Especially Bright Life's involvement and the attacks on Tara's apartment!

' No!' shouted the governor 'It can't be, they are my friends. They can't have caused so much havoc for a regime they helped put in office!'

As Dele tried to convince the governor, Tara was fidgety. The governor was reacting the way she had reacted when the news of her husband's death had been broken to her. He was trying to deny the fact even when he didn't have any alternative explanation. Dele's IC15 was with her. It occurred to her to check the whereabouts of the frog. What showed on the IC15 screen shocked her. She tapped Dele and handed it to him. Dele studied the screen and drew his gun. The CSO not knowing why also drew his gun. Dele pocketed the IC15 and edged towards the visitors' toilet in the hallway with his gun. The governor was about to start shouting when Dele threw open the toilet door. The frogs were already in the house! They jumped out and attacked. They seemed to be everywhere. Tara grabbed the nearest weapon she could find; a small stool. The governor who was shocked to the marrow screamed like a woman and dashed for the door. The door flew open as a servant who was being pursued by four frogs ran in. Ojeyemi fired at one of the frogs. There was a splash of red as the bullet dismembered the frog. Tara was swinging her stool wildly. Knocking out frog after frog. Dele and Ojeyemi shot the frogs with caution. They didn't want to waste bullets or shoot the governor, Tara or the servant. Luckily for them, Ojeyemi carried extra ammunition. One of the frogs went straight for the governor's right arm. Dele hit it off with the butt of his gun just in time before it could bite. It fell down unconscious. Tara remembered the virus. She struggled with the purse to get the syringe out. A frog landed on her back. Dele heard her scream. He spun her around and kicked the frog off her back.

In the chaos, the purse had fallen down. Tara crawled to where the purse was and opened it. It was right beside an unconscious frog. She pulled it out of the purse and stabbed the frog with it. As she injected the frog with the contents of the syringe, its eyes flicked open. She jumped back and the frog snapped, narrowly missing her hand.

The attack lasted about ten minutes. Many of the frogs had been injured or killed. The humans and frogs were battling for survival. All of a sudden, one of the frogs gave a loud croak. The frogs all retreated to the nearest water source; the water closet. They squeezed into it in a mass of black, white and pink.

Ojeyemi cautiously checked that they were all gone. The governor fell unconscious from the shock. Tara and Dele held each other. The blood was everywhere. The servant checked to see if the governor was still breathing. Eventually, the governor coughed and got back up. He looked at Dele and declared, 'Those bastards have to pay for this!'

'Yes sir, but how are we sure it's them?' Ojeyemi asked as he locked the toilet door for safety.

Dele kicked one of the dead frogs across the room and looked the Governor straight in the eye. 'I know how to find out,' he said.

＊　　　　　＊　　　　　＊

8.37 am. Sunday, July 27, 2060
The owners of Bright Life were happy. They were due to have a meeting with the governor. The attack on his house was going to make him act fast. Very soon, funds would be made available to them. Ali Hamza looked at his watch. The MT1 officer would soon be here. The Chika brothers were not around. That was unlike them and it made him slightly worried. They had gone to monitor the frogs. James and Mary seemed to be unconcerned about the absence of the brothers. They were involved in a private chat. He had heard the rumors of their affair but it didn't bother him. If she was having an affair with someone that young, good luck to her.

Suddenly, the brothers burst in. They looked angry and disoriented.
'All the frogs are dead!' shouted Ugo. 'Not a single one alive!'

Mary and James stopped chatting and watched the brothers as if they were expecting to hear that they had been 'April Fooled'. Hamza could not believe his ears. 'What happened?' He asked.

'We have not yet found the cause.' Answered Okey. 'We went in this morning and found them dead.'

Hamza was now feeling agitated. The frogs were engineered to withstand almost all threats. What could have happened? Was that why he had been uncomfortable all morning?

'Gentlemen, we need to comport ourselves. Very soon, we will be discussing with the governor. Let's try to look concerned. We will deal with this problem later.'

He had hardly finished his statement when the airbug came into view. Another one of those MT1 idiots was coming to check their monitor. They hurriedly tried to look composed. James let the man in. Surprisingly, the man did not salute. There was something familiar about him, James seemed to notice, but his mind was occupied with more important things. After all, the MT1 officials always came dressed the same way. The Bright Life officials were too pre-occupied with their thoughts to notice that while carrying out the security check, the MT1 man attached a small device to the screen.

*   *   *

The MT1 official got into his airbug and flew off. Once airborne, Dele took off his helmet and called the governor. 'Sir,' he exclaimed with a smile on his face, 'They are all yours!'

*   *   *

The screen came alive. The governor appeared. His arms were bandaged. He was looking bruised with a black left eye. He was holding a remote-control.

'Sir,' began Hamza 'we are very sorry for every...'

'Cut it!' ordered the governor. He looked angry and determined. 'I know about your silly experiments with those frogs. I am not like your average politician. I'm not ready to hear unnecessary stories. Just tell me the truth. Why did you do it?'

The room went silent. All five could not find a word. How did the governor find out? They looked at each other and seemed lost. Hamza, being the leader cleared his throat. There was no point feigning ignorance. It was time to come out clean.

'Governor, the company was running at a loss. All our inventions and innovations were not generating sales. There were too many home remedies in the market. We had to find an alternative source of income.'

'Do you know how many lives have been lost?' Asked the

governor. You have been undermining my government. I thought you people were my supporters. You have made my life miserable with the crisis you've caused! I even lost my daughter!'

Mary was staring at the ground. James was looking everywhere apart from the screen. Hamza watched the screen with a cold look on his face.

'To make omelets, you have to break a few eggs,' said Okey calmly. 'We regret the loss of your daughter and sincerely wish we could change things sir.'

'Rubbish! How many people lost their lives because of your stupid experiments?'

Ugo, who had lost his patience, shouted back 'Please forget this "holier than thou" attitude. If not for us, do you think you would have been in office? We set up the explosion to get you in there my friend!'

The governor looked like someone had poured ice cold water on him on a cold winter day. Even his black eye looked white. The realization of what had just been said hit him. He had been a pawn in their play. How much profit had they made all this while? They had been given tax breaks and research grants. Not to talk of construction funds for fixing the state after the nuclear disaster. Come to think of it, it was after he became governor that the company branched into engineering and construction!

'You are a bunch of murderers and you deserve to die!' Shouted the pale looking governor.

'It's not like that sir!' Shouted Mary sounding close to tears. 'It was Hamza and the brothers who came up with the idea.'
'And you went along with it so you are no different from

them. Say hello to Lucifer in hell!'

With that the governor pressed a button on the remote. The screen went blank. The number '10' appeared on the screen. A countdown began. It took a while for them to realise that they were witnessing the last few seconds of their lives. As the realisation hit them, all five scrambled for the door but it was too late. The explosion took out the penthouse of the building.

* * *

Tara and Dele lay in bed as they watched the news. Dele had refurbished the apartment. The explosion was widely reported. The governor promised to get to the root of the assassination of the 'Bright Life Five'. Condolence messages poured in. People expressed disgust at the way the five businessmen had been murdered.

'Why do you guys like blowing up everything?' asked Tara.

'I didn't do this one. You can ask the governor.'

She smiled, 'So what happens to the company?'

Dele smiled, 'There are many investors willing to buy the company. The explosion was not designed to destroy the company. It only took out the top management. There isn't much to worry about. Their future is still bright.'

* AMPHIBIAN ATTACK *

2.

ANIMALS ON THE RUN

BY

OKEY EGBOLUCHE

JULIO FOUND IT DIFFICULT TO BREATHE; it felt as if he was tied to his bed with several bricks on his chest. The end seemed near, he could not move any of his limbs. His felt numb.

Focus! Focus! He recalled Prof. Jagubar Obeidulah's psychology lessons, his tutor at the Mumbai Institute of Psychobiophysics. His wandering thoughts met at a point at which he concentrated on a higher level of existence, far above his present sense of captivity. He could faintly hear the music coming from the MP8 device in the room. His nerves were set free with a jolt as he lifted himself up. Breathing heavily, he touched the first button on his bed panel and a beam projected onto the wall. Manipulating the joy stick embedded in the panel, he clicked on 'time'; it was 5:30 am. Lagos time. He yawned and flipped the light sensor on.

What a night! He sighed. He had slept hugging his pillow tight. He longed to be with his heartthrob, Yinka. Good enough, she would join him that evening. The emptiness he had felt for the past few days was going to be filled with her presence.

Tall, slender, and graceful, he considered her the best thing that had happened to him. Most of his life after high school was spent in the laboratory; from one research project to another. And when he had almost concluded that he could never fall in love, their paths crossed and their friendship blossomed.

He had spent the last three days at the Marine Hotels in Lagos. He enjoyed the view of the ocean from his room in the hotel which was located offshore. Yinka, loved nature, so he hoped she was going to appreciate the panoramic beauty of the Eko Atlantic City from the glass walls of his hotel room. However, the beauty of the scenario did not compensate for the hectic nature of his work at the moment. He supervised over 120 online surveys coming from the joint academic partnership of Malaysian and Nigerian higher institutions. University of Ibadan was his centre.

Beep! Beep!! Beep!!! His pager signalled him. He pressed the middle button on the bed panel and its upper part bent upwards adjusting Julio to a sitting position. It was a reminder for the meeting he had at the university's robotics unit.

He finished his doctoral thesis six years earlier from the Mumbai Institute of Psychobiophysics with a summa cum laude in Psychophysics. His thesis on the Relativity of Bioengineered species received rave reviews in scientific journals. Not too long after, he was invited to become a guest lecturer at King Saud University in Riyadh, Saudi Arabia and the York School of Technology, Yorkshire, England. His country also wanted him. Celebrated as one of Nigeria's greatest minds in his field, Julio Akanchawa Ofia - who coincidentally is the great grandson of Dr. Roy Ofia, one of the inventors of the 'ogbunigwe' war machine which was widely used during the Nigeria- Biafra civil war - was part of the Lagos State Committee for Enhanced Robotics. Before then, he was part of Nigeria-Satcom12 project; which heralded the launch of Nigeria's twelfth satellite to space.

He was enjoying the attention from the Nigerian government, international groups and many youngsters who expressed their desire to venture into robotics because of his giant strides. Ironically, Yinka was not one of them. She was a biologist and she never minced words with Julio. She had always wanted him join the crusade to preserve nature. Julio often thought he was also helping humanity, albeit technologically. However, as the days rolled by, something about his passion for research in psychophysics was waning. 'Could it be because of my love for this woman?' he asked himself. It was something he kept only to himself.

At his instruction, the hotel's auto messenger device rolled a table with his favourite breakfast over to him. As he ate, he recollected his last meeting with the Mayor of Lagos who expressed his interest in curbing the population explosion constantly plaguing Lagos. Now rated as the world's most populous city, the mega-city's rise in world prominence was unequalled.

Lagos had its fair share of the good as well as the ugly. It had the largest movie making industry in the world. It had the most robust stock market and was still a place where the cheapest labour could be found in the world- a position it contested with Dakkah in Bangladesh. It had also become notorious for a booming sex industry, piracy and crime. Yet in the last thirty years, two winners of the Nobel Prize for literature and three winners of the Booker Prize had emerged from the city in addition to several winners of other notable literary prizes such as the Caine Prize for African Writing, Commonwealth Prize and Global Awareness Genius Award for Literature.

Twenty minutes later, his roadable aircraft took off from the hotel's hanger. He loved his automobile. He was one of the privileged few that could afford such a luxury in Lagos. After about twenty minutes in the air; he descended to a landing stop on the outskirts of Lagos, joining other cars on the highway.

Ibadan meant many things to Julio, the fondest being the city of delicious Amala and Ewedu soup. He relished the memories of his last visit to one of the leading restaurants in the city where he was served by one of the most beautiful ladies he had ever seen. The waitresses paced around in G-strings, dangling their firm and well-rounded boobs as they took customers' orders. Their voluptuous breasts, were all thanks to enhanced breast surgery techniques. He felt a tinge of satisfaction as he watched them walk. He felt fulfilled, but he did not know if it was because of the delicious meal of Amala or because of the beautiful girls. "Enough of robots! Nothing feels as good as being served by my fellow human." He said as he tipped a smiling waitress.

As the cars crowded into mild traffic at the checkpoint on the Lagos Ibadan expressway, he quickly placed his order using his mobile. Connecting the bluetooth of his mobile device with his car printer, he got a hard copy of the receipt. He smiled and mumbled, "I will give it to one of the waitresses as soon as I get there." He wished the restaurant would allow the girls interact more with the customers and perhaps touch them too. "21st century business has gone nuclear," he remarked, giggling. His soliloquy was interrupted by sudden pandemonium.

Cars were honking their horns; a few flying machines similar to his were taking off. Motorbikes and pedestrians were making U-turns and racing back to the other lane of the highway where Julio was. They made signs to other oncoming automobiles not to continue in that direction. Shouts of, "Turn back!" "No go there!" "Wahala! Wahala!" filled the air. Julio quizzically looked the way of the car on his left and he discovered that the mulatto occupant also wore an inquisitive and worried look.

"I hope it is not a robbery scene." The man said, despair written all over his face.

"Me too. It would be worse if it is a tremor but I presume it can't happen in this part of the country." Julio replied.

"A planet in peril."

"We can only do our lot to save mother earth." Julio answered him, looking at his rear-view mirror wondering what the automobiles behind him were doing. The car on his right was operated by a robot. He hissed when he noticed it. To worsen his ill feelings at the moment, the robot was a product of Nitech, an American company. He knew them when he saw them. He disliked the West.

"Good morning roboo" he said turning to the right.

"Good morning friend" the robot replied. Its vibration sensor showed that it was sensing some unusual happenings as regards the relationship between field and space.

In a few minutes, Julio found himself on the other side of the highway, racing back with others. He was not surprised when a text message appeared on his car's audio visual device signalling him to cancel the trip because of an unusual uprising at the Lagos-Ibadan expressway.

"That was so nice of the Information Service Unit of the University." He whispered. "I have always told them that there would be changes if a human being was appointed to man it. The guys are doing a great job there." He said, nodding his head.

He tuned to the local radio station expecting to hear breaking news that would help him clarify what had actually gone wrong. After ten minutes with no information on the situation, he switched on the TV button. The news highlight, mentioned the occurrence but promised to give more details in a short while. As he pressed the remote control to switch on the laser disc player, his pager beeped. He had set it in the answering machine mode earlier. The call was from Yinka. He allowed it ring without picking. He knew she would drop a message. He loved hearing her husky voice.

"Honey pie, I hope you are safe. I just heard about a major disturbance on the outskirts of Lagos, very close to Ibadan. Please let me know where you are. I can't wait to see you. I would be at the airport in an hour. I miss you so much."

Hearing Yinka's voice excited him and calmed his nerves. Julio never told Yinka that he had been trying to mix a voice similar to hers in a robot. He had been able to build a voice that could be said to be Yinka's into one of the robots in the Laboratory. After he did that, he brought taped versions of Yinka's voice and the one he built and placed tracks of them at random in the amplifier. He decided to choose which was Yinka's or the robot's voice. He was annoyed he never made any wrong choice as he was still able to differentiate them. His assistants did not get it right like he did as they could not

47

differentiate the voices when they were subjected through the examinations, yet he felt he was yet to mix Yinka's voice properly.

Back in Lagos, he was glad to hear that flights would resume for aeroplanes and air jets passing through the Lagos-Ibadan airspace. Nothing was going to disrupt Yinka's travel plan.

A boy of about ten years stopped beside his vehicle, displaying his wares. He had agidi and moi-moi. He called the boy's attention. He loved it when moi-moi was wrapped with local leaves. Dieticians believed it was healthier than the type that was wrapped with foil or the increasingly popular recycled optic paper. No wonder it cost a lot more. Julio never forgot what he read in his Grandmother's diary where she said the leaves even added more nutrients and flavour to the moi-moi. After buying two wraps, he continued his journey as he veered off Ikorodu Road towards Lagos mainland where everything seemed normal.

The city was unusually calm. There were just a few hawkers at the Oshodi Bridge. It suddenly dawned on him that he needed to charge his car. The nearest charge station was about 10 minutes away.

He got to the station, parked his car beside one of the available charge points. He paid for the 1.5 KV/30 minutes category. While he waited, the ongoing conversation between the attendants caught his attention.

"Dem say Mayor don approve say make every school child dey use microchip."

"Haba, I think say that microchip na only for security people."

"Kabakablass, who talk so? This one na to enable parents monitor their children."

"Children don too spoil, their waka too much."

"Na wa o! E fit help o!" The lady attendant replied turning to meet Julio's gaze. She winked at him and proceeded to do her job of checking the cars at the charge points.

Julio looked at her as she walked. She looked sexy in her high heel boots and unbuttoned overalls which she revealed her skimpy dress. He wondered why ladies were so crazy about piercings; the lady had about four on each ear, one on each eyebrow, one on the lower lip and another on her tongue. The craze for piercing was so much that popular celebrities and new wave female preachers had a lot to show. Yinka was different; she just had one on each ear.

As he went to pick a can of soft drink from the vending machine, he noticed a neat and well-maintained 2015 model of Toyota Camry. He was amazed and excited. The owner had grey hairs and was possibly in his late sixties or early seventies. The car was one that Julio had always wanted to have for keeps. He noticed something interesting about the occupant; he looked very much like Desmond Eliot, the octogenarian Nollywood and Hollywood star.

As Julio turned the keys of the door to his charged automobile, his eyes moved to the videosonic board close to the charge station. A bold inscription by the neon lights caught his attention, "Let's speak more in our mother tongue. We are fast losing our heritage." He turned and smiled at the attendant when he saw the name, Iphie on her tag. The lady smiled back. Iphie was a funkified way of writing Ify, the short form of the name, Ifeoma or Ifeyinwa. She was also Igbo.

"Kedu ka I mere?" Julio asked her in Igbo.

"Whatever! I am fine," the stunned attendant answered, suddenly changing her countenance. She frowned and chewed the gum in her mouth provocatively.

Julio gladly pocketed a five afro bill that he had wanted to give her as a tip. He became worried that advances in technology could be the reason many young people now detest communicating in their native languages. As he veered his car off the station, he was thankful that even though he had the best western education from the east he could still understand his mother tongue, even if he was not fluent in it.

✳✳✳✳✳✳✳✳

The arrival lounge of the Murtala Mohammed International Airport was busy. Many Nigerians were arriving from Dubai and Rio de Janeiro. There were also many Chinese and Indians who were the controllers of commerce in Lagos. Their Nigerian based companies were booming and exporting products to various parts of the world. Julio saw only a few Arabs, who walked proudly in their thobes, gutra and igals. They invested heavily in arable and livestock farming in Nigeria. He wondered why Nigeria did not colonise other smaller African countries; after all, it had the needed power and might.

He looked up and saw Yinka trying to get her luggage from the conveyor belt. He smiled as he watched the robot carrying her luggage walk out of the lobby with her. He moved to the exit door that Yinka would take. As soon as Yinka saw him, she rushed into his arms. They kissed passionately and held on to each other. The robot stopped and waited while an elderly woman passing by stood distracted as she stared at the duo. The woman's daughter turned back when she could not see her mother by her side. She rushed to her mother and poked her. The old woman shook her head and said loudly:

"Awon omode asiko yi ti ba aiye je, Eko ki'ise ilu Oyibo."* People who understood what she said laughed. Some others were irritated by her utterance.

"What's that grandma woman saying, Mum?" a girl of about five years asked as she tugged at her Mum, pointing to the elderly woman.

"Toyin, she is thanking God for arriving safely from London." The Mother replied.

"God? Oh! Mum, but she looks angry. God would ignore an angry prayer, init?"

"Toyin, hurry up, roboo is waiting for us." The mother obviously did not have an answer to her question.

"Spark, the roboo!" the little girl smiled, "I missed him."

Julio carried Yinka in both arms, unaware of the reactions around them. The robot followed them as they moved. Ten minutes later, they were in the air as Julio flew the car to Marine Hotels at the Eko

Atlantic City.

✳✳✳✳✳✳✳✳

Julio met Yinka about a year earlier at the public complaints office of Mumbai International Airport, when they both had problems with their bookings. He liked her immediately and could not resist a word or two with her. She too was eagerly waiting for a compliment or greeting from him. After all, she was looking her best that day. When it seemed as if the young man was more bothered about his flight problem than noticing her, she had summoned courage and was about to ask him a question about Tata Airlines to which she already knew the answer, when he broke the ice. Their conversation flowed, broken only by slight stuttering and anxious pauses. They exchanged their phone and online contacts. From that day, they chatted online from time to time.

His visit to her in Hyderabad was a memorable one. She took him out for a meal of Paneer Tikka and Maharashtrian Chicken Curry. He never liked spicy food but he had no other option but to eat the food without any complaints to make his host comfortable.

"Eight glasses of water a day, keeps the doctor away," Julio said as he took a third cup of water.

"No wonder you've been drinking."

"Yeah, I want to live long, you know."

"You won't live that long when the food isn't this peppery." She giggled.

"Yinka, how do you mean?" Julio asked gleefully.

"Sure, you'll drink less water if the food isn't this spicy." They both laughed. Julio laughed louder and it made the Indians in the restaurant look their way. One of them made eye contact with Julio and he laughed too. The man kept nodding his head as he laughed and Julio stopped laughing wondering what was amusing the man.

"Yinka, that guy over there is laughing with us," Jullio said. Yinka burst out laughing again and he joined her too. Now, it was time for the Indian to wonder. He stopped laughing and stared at

Julio and Yinka.

Julio left the restaurant happy. He had a good laugh and a full stomach, though he had to whistle lightly to douse the peppery feel on his tongue. He looked forward to a good time with Yinka's pets when they got home.

Yinka had a set of mice at her apartment. She was so attached to them that she had a profile of each of them on the old and reliable Facebook social network. She weighed them twice a day as part of her research; her aim was to determine the chromosomes responsible for their conformity to changes in the environment. Julio called them, her pets.

As Julio's fondness for Yinka grew, so did his fondness for her weekly column, 'We are Nature', in *Mumbai Mirror* also grow. In one of Yinka's essays she argued:

"The increasing habitat loss, introduced species, over-exploitation and pollution, all caused by human activities, combined with stochastic factors place ever-increasing pressure on natural populations had continuously affected animal populations. Rats and mice are like man. They move with the changing times. It is not unusual to find a rat even in the tallest sky scrapers in any part of the world. Researchers have taken them successfully on various space missions."

Julio had started to deeply appreciate animals and mankind. He was of the opinion that man should concentrate more on saving his kind instead of investing heavily on machinery and robotics. But for the huge amount he received as monthly wage from the Lagos State Government, he would have declined the offer to be part of the Lagos State Committee for Enhanced Robotics.

While he looked forward to settling down with this enigma of a lady-Yinka- who had become the love of his life; he remembered how his last meeting with Baba, her father had gone awry.

****

Julio woke up, to find Yinka backing him as she sat on the bed with all her attention focused on her pager. He peeped to see what she was doing. He was not surprised when he found out she was having her confession. A catholic priest was online. I wonder if these priests are ever tired of hearing sins, he thought. He walked into the bathroom to have a shower. A cool refreshing bath was what he always called it. He needed it at a time the heavens pelted the earth with so much heat from the sun. The ozone layer was even kinder when compared to what analysts had said several years earlier.

"Ekaro ololufe mi," Julio said when he stepped out of the bathroom. Yinka smiled.

"Ututuoma ina anyi," Yinka replied. They greeted each other in the other person's language.

"I've always told you it's not ina ayi, its nna anyi."

"Okay, nna anyi."

"That's better," Julio replied, "But, meanwhile, I am not your father, call me obi m and not nna anyi."

"Hey ya, Julio, I've heard nna anyi in your home videos."

"That was to depict how it happened in the past, when wives called their husbands father in respect, baby." Julio said squeezing his face," We are in the robotic age now, you know."
Yinka frowned and Julio immediately knew why she did.

"But that's how I get paid and the world needs my service more than ever," Julio said, but he only managed to infuriate Yinka. She stared into his eyes and said, "a planet in peril."

"We can only do our lot to save mother earth." Julio managed to reply. He remembered he was meant to visit Yinka's father in two days' time. Yinka's countenance had changed and he chose not to raise the issue right then. The quiet room needed some laughter once again.

Julio instructed the auto-messenger device and it rolled a cup of coffee to him. He sipped from the cup, turning to Yinka, he smiled. "You care for a drink?" He asked, knowing what reaction to expect.
Yinka turned away; she hissed, rolled her eyes and moved her head back to Julio's smiling face. She smiled back, "you'd better do what you ought to do." She said.

"Choco is her favourite!" He exclaimed and moments later a

cup of chocolate drink was rolled to him. He took the cup, kissed it and passed it to Yinka. Julio caressed her back with his left hand as she sipped the drink.

"Now tell me, what you told that priest?" He asked mischievously.

"My sins, of course!"

"Your sins? Get a life baby. You sin?"

"Yeah, I told him we had online sex several times and you bore all for me on the web cam." She said sarcastically and they both laughed.

"Common that's online. No physical contact. And don't forget you denied me the real thing last night."

"Naughty boy," Yinka replied giggling.

"Kabakablass" Julio remarked, "You know I am a good guy." And they giggled even more.

But Julio's thoughts darted to Baba again. He had to talk about what was bothering him.

"Baby, do you think Baba would have changed his mind about me?"

Yinka sighed and moved closer to him.

"Baby, he needs to know that I am human." He continued, "I have regards for all. I am not a destroyer, rather I enhance life. I do what I do because my knowledge and services are needed. And that is what I have known how to do best, all my life."

"Baba does not detest you," Yinka said, "It's just that he has passed through a lot. His arable farming outsourcing firm crumbled because of the advent of robotic farming. His father's landed property at Elekon was acquired by the government for the nuclear plant."

Julio had heard this several times. As much as he would have preferred Yinka to have a mind of her own and take her decisions irrespective of what her father thought, he felt awkward because, by her training and passions she was also an environmentalist.

"My father is not being selfish. His stance has a lot to do with his religious beliefs. I know he likes you as a person but he is being cautious."

Religion was the last thing Julio needed to hear. It is everybody's personal business and should not affect their dealings with others. It was not a good enough reason. Some ladies well known in religious circles that advocated one man-one wife still got contractually married to men, sometimes at a ratio of two or three to one man.

"I love you, Julio and I always will, no matter the challenge we might go through in convincing Baba. I will stand by you."

Julio held her arms; she was one woman in a million. Women were gaining the upper hand in most spheres of the society and so they increasingly became insolent and bossy. The men did not mind because many women paid their bills. Yinka was different. She had a good job, she was well paid but she chose to be submissive to him. He appreciated the kind of upbringing that Baba gave her. He understood why she meant a lot to the old man. Yinka deeply cared for her father. She had lost her mother at an early age and Baba was the only one that was there for her.

"I love you, Yinka," Julio replied.

Julio gave her a passionate and warm embrace and she melted in his arms. They caressed each other and when Julio was about to take it further, she shrugged him off. "What is it this time?" Julio asked, breathing heavily.

"Look," Yinka replied, pointing at the TV's projected beam on the wall. It was the news. Julio's erect manhood shrunk when he directed his gaze to the wall.

****

"This is crap," Julio said holding on tightly to Yinka. "We raced back to Lagos because a bunch of crazy animals invaded the roads? If the conservation authorities couldn't find what chased them out of the bush, they should have hunted them down. We all need meat, don't we?"

Yinka did not reply. Her eyes glued to the projection on the

wall. Julio bent his head to observe why she was silent. He immediately knew she was unhappy. He gently caressed her nape, chin and shoulders. He kissed her on her cheeks. He could smell the gel on her jerry curled hair. As he touched the screen on the bed panel to increase the room temperature, he felt something wet at the back of his left hand, Yinka's tears.

He resisted the urge to ask if everything was okay. Something was definitely wrong. He wanted to flick the TV beam off but he decided to allow her interest in the news wane first. It was obvious her reactions had a lot to do with the news about the animals on rampage. "Tell me about it," he said. Yinka shrugged and Julio loosened his grip. She gently moved away from his arms to lay beside him. Julio flicked the beam off. He lay down too. "What is it, honey?" he asked.

"Eko oni baje" Yinka replied him in a whisper. She curled herself up still sobbing.

Julio knew that love making would no longer be part of the night. Yinka's fanatical love for the preservation of Lagos bothered him. What did a bunch of insane animals have to do with him?

He got up from the bed to concentrate on the work he still had to do. He fixed up a shisha, and inhaled a puff, feeling his head expand and contract. It was a habit he learnt from his Saudi friends in Riyadh.

He tapped his pager screen and read a mail from Abia State University asking him if he would be available to be a keynote speaker at the flagging off ceremony of the academic exchange programme between the institution and the University of Malaysia, Perlis. "I hope these guys get it right, like the Zaria and Nilai folks," he said.

＊＊＊＊＊＊＊＊＊＊＊

Julio found a comfortable seat at the reception in Baba's house. He could faintly hear Baba and the students communicate in his study. He hoped the old man would remember he had asked him to see him. He brought out his pager, touched the ticker on his timeline and checked his updates. While two updates each were from King Saud University, Riyadh and Mumbai Institute of Psychobiophysics, the only one left was from *Mumbai Mirror*, Yinka's article for the weekly column; 'We Are Nature' had just been published.

Yinka had left Julio's hotel room earlier to meet her father. She assured him she was going to put things in place for his coming. But she called him later to tell him that Baba would have some visitors- high school student members of the Environmental Friendly Club of King's College Lagos. They gave Baba short notice about their coming. Being a patron of the club, he did not decline.

"Please, that should not stop you from still keeping to time dear." Yinka chuckled.

"Today na today," Julio smiled. "I have conditioned my mind that I would see Baba and sort things out once and for all."

"Thanks dear. Just find a way and keep yourself busy while I go and get things from the hypermarket nearby."

He scanned through the article and a paragraph caught his attention:

"*There are several changes on the planet that have made life miserable for various species. While domesticated animals are not as badly affected because of the increase in livestock farming, others are suffering. There is an increase in number of endangered species. Animals are fast losing their habitat because of the destruction of forests.*"

"It is logical. She is making a point," he whispered. He shifted on the seat as his eyes probed the article further.

"*There is a great deal of animal migration going on. We have sacrificed their habitations for money. The Eastern and Western worlds are competing to invest in our arable land and we are dancing to their tune because of the huge amounts of money involved. Decades ago, our crude oil was our albatross and a particular region of this country had their water bodies polluted. They cried for the right to control their resources but they were only given the kind of control they sought when their oil wells were drying up. Today they are left bitter and battered. Their land cannot support any crops.*"

Loud ovation from the study interrupted his concentration. He read the paragraph again. She was referring to Nigeria. "Naija!" he whispered and sighed. But her comments about Lagos further aroused his interest.

"Their misfortune contributed to the migration to Lagos; O yes! Just like the unfortunate animals, people trooped to Lagos. From the South where they could not cultivate their lands because it was acidic, they could not fish because their fishes had long been dead. People also came from the North, the very rich north currently enjoying mechanised agriculture courtesy of robotics. Many lost their jobs because the robots did the farming. And even the food that their lands yielded were sold away for huge foreign exchange. Lagos was their last hope. If the animals could read and write, maybe they would come to Lagos too-the land of promise and centre of excellence."

"Now she is bringing in too much emotion, no way!"

"And it has become the most populous city in the world. The beautiful flowers it was known for, over 50 years ago are no longer there. The bare lands that should be beautified are now farms... I wonder why government establishments would use robots when people still need jobs. Is this an achievement?"

He could not read any further, he rolled down to the comments section and typed: *'The state is not slacking at all in its developmental efforts. The government may have made mistakes in the past but I marvel when I see the skyscrapers, (new trend) and green houses in new Lagos. They are comparable to the ones you see in other developed places. Robots may cost a lot initially but it saves cost in the long run. We are moving along with the times. We control the African market in many sectors.'* He refused to write his name in the comment.

Julio could still hear low tones from the discussion going on in Baba's study. He wondered what had kept them so long. He walked to the door that led to the study and could hear them clearly. He looked through the glass and he could see all of them in the room. Baba was passionate about what he talked to the children about. He was seated resting his back on the cushion of his adjustable bed. The students sat around him on the floor in a fashion that reminded Julio of the videos of NTA's *Tales by Moonlight* that were given to him by his grandfather when he was six. His grandfather told him, he enjoyed watching it as a schoolboy.

"I cannot farm again. Government has taken my land. They said they are interested in agriculture and yet hunger looms. They are exporting cash crops." He rubbed his arms and thought about what next to say. "When we were younger, our country had a lot of crude oil capable of making us so rich, but they wasted it. The West helped them waste it. Today our oil wells have dried up. Even those that have been newly discovered are of little use." He coughed and readjusted his spectacles.

Julio's mind wandered to the stories his father told him about how Nigeria bounced back from bankruptcy, poverty, economic turmoil and a crisis that almost led to a second civil war when the world stopped using fossil fuels. The government which was still basking in the euphoria of discovering crude oil in the Chad Basin after the oil wells of the Niger Delta had almost dried up was caught unawares by the development. The can-do spirit and never-say-die attitude of his countrymen moved the nation forward again. He still gave his ears to what Baba was saying.

"They said our oil pollutes the air. Now they also use our crops to produce fuel while we have little remaining for us to feed on. Lagos is able to pay social security to young people. What about other states incapable of doing so? Our youths have become lazy because they are paid even when they don't work and food is expensive."

Baba added, "I think most of our problems began when we started building houses on top of water."

Julio frowned, enthusiastically waiting for what next Baba had to say. Offshore hotels were his favourite lodging place.

"I like sea fish, Babs." One of the students said.

"Don't call me Babs, I have always told you to call me Baba."

"Come on Babs. Baba sounds old fashioned, that's what they called Jide Kosoko in the home videos, donkey years ago. I love you and I'll never make you look bad." The students laughed at the boy's comment.

Baba hinted that the session was over and told the students

to wait for some refreshment. His stood up, looking like an Arab in his robe. Julio tiptoed back to the reception.

＊＊＊＊＊＊＊＊

Julio did not find it out of place to bow before an elderly man in respect, but found it amusing as he was told he needed to lie prostrate on the floor instead, when he greeted Baba.

Baba was passionate about preserving African culture and the symbols and monuments that represented them.

"Young people have been so inundated with other cultures that prostrating before elders has become a thing of the past. The best you can get from a kid these days is a wave and 'Hi Dad' or 'Hi Uncle' greeting. You would be lucky to get an accompanying smile." Baba would say.

Julio remembered his visit to a British family originally from Ondo State, Nigeria at their apartment in Granada Compound, Riyadh. He was so impressed at how his host's kids prostrated as they greeted him. He commended his hosts for bringing up their children the African way. Their mother was all smiles and boasted, "Of course! It's my duty to instil respect in them."

On his subsequent visit, to his astonishment he only received a 'Hi Uncle' greeting from the kids. Some months later, he was not surprised that he was the one to greet the kids first.

Here he was now, before a man who was an advocate of a lifestyle his people had already done away with.

"Hello Julio," I hope I did not keep you waiting for too long. Baba's deep but shaky voice did not catch Julio unawares.

"Good afternoon. Not at all Sir. I kept myself busy with my pager here." Julio replied, prostrating as soon as he saw the old man. He felt out of place and did not find it funny when Baba did not reply. He stood up only to find out that the old man had walked past him, so he quietly followed Baba as he walked out of the reception.

"I got to know that it was your grandfather that built the

letter bomb, widely believed to have been used by a former military head of state to murder the journalist, Deju Cole?"

Baba's unexpected comment shook Julio as he sat down on one of the sofas in the parlour. He bent his head dejectedly. It was a true fact but it was something he kept to himself. The only time the issue was ever raised was in a discussion with his tutor, Prof. Jagubar Obeidullah. He had thought the Nigerian press would dig out the information when he was named a member of the Lagos State Commission for Enhanced Robotics but they never did. Baba fixed his gaze on him expecting a reply. He had to say something.

"Baba, I asked my Dad about it after a cousin raised the issue and he told me that my Grandpa never accepted or denied the allegation after it was widely published in news magazines in 1994." Baba did not seem satisfied with his reply. He scratched his grey hairs and said, "Yours is a family of scientists."

"Yes Baba," Julio replied, "

"Scientists indeed!" Baba said sarcastically.

"Well, my Dad is a social scientist," he replied hoping to change the tone of the discussion.

"I have no reservations about your relationship with my daughter. What I am concerned about is this your family history of explosives and scientific destruction. I am even more uncomfortable with your field considering your antecedents."

Julio was dumbfounded. He wondered if Yinka had made any effort to convince Baba about him. He was afraid a reply from him may further infuriate the man.

"I understand your concerns, Baba," he managed to say.

"You do not!" Baba blurted out, "I care for my daughter. I want the best for her."

"I care for her too," Julio almost tearfully replied, looking at Baba.

"If you do, then stop wasting humanity and our world."

He had to say something. "Baba, I was trained to be a robotic scientist, I do what I do to make life better...to uplift mankind, to provide easier ways of doing things, to.."

"Then stay away from us!" Baba cut in.

"Baba..Bab..a." Julio stammered kneeling down before the old man.

"Do not Baba me," the old man replied; "I need some peace."

Julio stood up, disappointed. He did not know whether to wait for Yinka or not. But he knew he was going to have trouble sleeping later in the night.

****

Another isolated case of rampaging animals at Badagry had just been reported. Julio watched the news on LTV immediately after the incident. He could see the worried victims who were either injured or had their valuables destroyed. He studied one of the wrecked cars and was convinced it was the Toyota model he had always wanted to keep as an antique. He could hear various versions of what happened as the people talked in loud voices.

The reporter moved to interview another witness. The witness looked familiar, to Julio's surprise, it was the elderly man he saw at the charge station, the Desmond Elliot look-alike.

"What a shame!" Julio said.

He could hear his pager beep. He reached for it. Yinka was calling. He quietly replaced the device. She must have followed the report; he did not want to hear her cry once again. He needed to think.

That the streets of Lagos would be taken over by homeless animals was something nobody would have imagined 30 years ago. Animals roaming aimlessly in the streets, charging at residents and moving in large groups.

Various interpretations have been given to the occurrences. The most notable were by evangelists who ascribed it to the end of times. Some traditionalists believed that the god of thunder was angry, while others attributed it to the dearth of hunters. The most interesting explanation came from the National Geographic Channel who affirmed that the Lagos Mega City infrastructural development project including the Eko Atlantic City was carried out years ago without adequate plans for the maintenance of the ecosystem.

Already, across Nigeria, the 'A Planet in Peril' campaign was gaining momentum. Several groups uncomfortable with the increasing job losses and pay cuts in the country were calling for the abolition of robots in the job place and all public places.

A team of panellists were on TV to discuss the issue. Julio had declined to be part of such discourse on the NN24 news channel and LTV in the past.

****

Julio could not hide his restlessness as he made several attempts to reach the Government House. The Governor's aides were not co-operative and his emails, text and satellite messages were not replied.

He was perturbed by the recent developments in the state.

He stared at the headline of the Sun newspaper, two days later.

BIZZARE!!!
Rampaging Animals Kill Lagos Deputy Governor.

He knew it was time to resign from the Lagos State Committee for Enhanced Robotics.

****

As Lagosians discussed the tragedy that befell the State, Julio found a quiet time to draft a statement for the media:

Owing to the blatant disregard for the preservation of wildlife and shunning of all attempts by me to reach the state on the issue, I hereby tender my resignation as a member of the Lagos State Commission for Enhanced Robotics.

Many may be of the opinion that my assignment in the committee had little to do with the conservation of our natural resources, but I wish to state

clearly that I am human and I have feelings for fellow biological beings.
Technology is an asset to mankind and should be used for the
advancement and preservation of life . In the case of Lagos State and sadly
Nigeria, it has increasingly turned out to be the greatest obstacle to the existence
of life in our lands, water bodies and air...'

The development was a major highlight in the news aired by AIT,
NTA, SABC, AfroTV and CNN. It was another blow to the
technological advancement enthusiasts and the State. In a counter
move, the spokesperson for the Lagos State Government issued a
statement condemning the resignation of Dr Julio Akanchawa at a
time the state was in grief owing to the attack on the Deputy
Governor's convoy by rampaging buffalos which led to her demise.

"*Dr. Julio Akanchawa has displayed his insensitivity to the plight of the*
Lagos State Government which just lost one of its most eminent citizens.
Condemning a state government that has made giant strides in making sure that
the state grows in leaps and bounds technologically along with their counterparts
in more developed regions of the world is a disappointing show of short
sightedness.
While the state government has not received his alleged resignation
letter, the government would willingly accept his resignation and seek more
focused minds to beef up the committee as soon as the four days of mourning are
over."

Julio had appeared on BBC's *Straight Talk* an hour before the
statement from Pedro.

****

The state governor was filled with remorse as he stood before the
press corps. His media assistant had earlier talked to the men of the
press that it was not a time for questions but a time to join forces
with the state government to remove fear and instil hope in the
people. Having been invited for a meeting with the governor which

was to take place in an hour, Julio was told by the governor's aides to join the media briefing. He wanted to hide his face when the Laser T130 100mm focused its beam where he sat but he resisted the urge. He believed that some die-hard reporters would want to hear from him as soon as the briefing was over and he would willingly oblige them no matter the security barrier. If it was the governor's ploy to win cheap popularity from the masses by using his presence against him as propaganda, he was ready to thwart it.

He did not hear the governor's opening words because he busy updating his Twitter, Facebook and Orion timelines. He messaged his department in Riyadh, Yorkshire, Mumbai and Ibadan telling them about his invitation to Alausa emphasising that he believed it was a mission to mend fences with the government but they should monitor any development in case the government had other plans.

When he looked up to concentrate on what the governor was saying, the intensity of the camera flashes from the paparazzi as they took shots of him, made him realise that he did the right thing by contacting his associates. No doubt, a picture of him in Government House would adorn the front pages of newspapers and online news magazines later in the day. Lucas Otedola-Phillips, the man he had suddenly developed a disliking for, spoke with passion.

"...We, as true agents of change and positive development would no longer allow our quest to grow with global trends to undermine our existence. Our ecosystem, which has suffered abuse as a result of neglect and wrong priorities in the hands of my administration and other governments of the past is, fast degrading and increasingly throwing us into a state of natural imbalance. While the developed world, the new power blocs and emerging nations had made adequate provisions for the preservation of their vegetation and wildlife, we followed them blindly in an aggressive quest for technological advancement. Thus, our national pride-the buffalos, orangutans, lions and antelopes that made the West and East envy us have been rendered fugitives in their own land, how much more trees, shrubs, plants and sea population that play roles in one way or the other in the food chain?" There was silence in the room as the governor spoke.

****

Yinka cried as she listened to the governor. She sobbed not because of the recent alarming events but because the government had woken up from its slumber.

Baba kept nodding his head, "Better late than never," he said repeatedly.

****

"My administration is committed to the preservation of nature. The term 'endangered species' which seemed to have been wiped away from our priorities will be fully re-instated and respected. We take responsibility for every contrary action we took in the past and crave your understanding. Now, more than ever, we seek your support in our drive to make our environment safe and habitable for all. We would cut our spending on robotics, nuclear technology and space missions while we increase our support for the State Environmental Maintenance Authority, the Conservation Foundation and Non-Governmental Agencies involved in the preservation of our environment. The publicity drive 'A Planet in Peril- Save Mother Earth' would be stepped up. It would no longer be mere rhetoric but a call for action and our new lifestyle."

"If we do not act now, then we are rendering the Earth inhabitable for generations unborn. The future is not far away, the future is now, every passing minute and second. Every breath of our life, every action we take and decisions we make sum up the future'."

The governor paused and there was thunderous ovation.

"My administration would set up a high powered committee that will liaise with the relevant bodies and map out strategies to get us back on the right track in choosing the right priorities in our mode of operation and preservation of our natural populations. It is worthy to note that the guru of robotics and a reliable resource person in our technological drive but now turned nature activist, Dr Julio Akanchawa would be part of the committee. More details about..."

Another resounding ovation drowned out the governor's voice. Julio wondered why he had to mention his name. He had not even been briefed about such a committee but when he saw all the pressmen and government aides stand up as they applauded, he knew he was not going to say no.

His pager was busy with incoming congratulatory and solidarity messages. Among all the incoming calls he only picked the call from his head of department in Mumbai and Yinka's.

"I am happy for you," Yinka said, her husky voice tingling with love for Julio.

"Thanks Yinka. Frankly, I feel that you are more suited for this committee than me. It's your field, your passion and what you have hoped for."

"I know darling but you are the one the whole world knows. Don't worry, I would always be by your side and give you every support."

****

Julio was at the State Air Mission's dressing room. Moments later he was all dressed up. He could feel the weight of the air bag that was attached to his bullet proof jersey. Governor Otedola-Phillips was dressed likewise. He did not know when the governor removed his adire agbada. Julio and the Governor were given a few lessons about altitude and maintaining balance in the air. He wondered why they could not just use a helicopter instead of a mini dreamliner air jet.
The Z111 unit air marshals were fully kitted and he could see their laser cellular ipads and magnum 125 guns. The satellite messaging device had already been installed on the air jet and they were called to come on board. The Governor's aide waited for them to move in before he came on board. Inside the aircraft, he could see that some other eminent people were seated too. Surprisingly, he could make

out the face of Ata Mensah, the CNN correspondent for West Africa who waved at him as he sat down.

The take-off was smooth and the air jet moved over the forests that bordered Lagos. They could observe wildlife from the screen in their seats. The laser magnifying camera attached to the craft made it seem as if they were close to the animals and plants. There was a herd of cattle moving westwards, they were racing towards the borders of Benin Republic and there was no herdsman with them. They also flew above crows. The birds flapped their wings quacking and moving without a purpose or direction because barely fifteen minutes after they saw them moving north east, they all changed their direction to the south. Obviously, it was not the air jet that scared them because it had the most modern silencer in its 15-cylinder engine. They could also see the land mass allocated to the wealthy Al-Omair family of Bahrain for integrated rubber and cocoa plantation. Work was going on there as trees were being felled and their trunks uprooted from the soil in the forest.

They saw corpses of chimpanzees... a sorry sight. They saw the Elekon nuclear plant, located a few kilometres from the dead chimpanzees. More buffalos were still on the run. They could see that they were already heading towards Seme. The communications officer of the air mission quickly alerted the République du Bénin Service De Police and the Beninoise Interior Minister. Hundreds of antelopes stood still before the Lagos Lagoon. The animals were not drinking water from the lagoon which showed that they stood still because the water was an obstacle to their run. The men quickly alerted the National Conservation Foundation Headquarters in Abuja and the State Conservation Authority. The animal scientist in their midst remarked that if the herbivores were not evacuated to a more friendly environ where they could feed on grass and be safe from predators, they may start dying of hunger, get drowned if the water overflows or get attacked by predators.

Julio was opportune to appreciate wildlife and nature as he saw aerial views of beautiful landscapes and seascapes. Their sojourn ended when the director of Air Missions signalled that the Ogun

State control tower had sent word that they were almost veering into their air space without any prior clearance. The governor requested that they flew back to the Alagbon airstrip.

As they all alighted from the aircraft, Julio's pager beeped. It was a text message from Yinka:

Baba is so proud of you. He can't wait to see your people. In fact, he has started referring to you as 'my son-in-law'.

Julio smiled; he was glad about the development and proud to be part of the remarkable drive to save the animals on the run.

TRANSLATIONS

"Awon omode asiko yi ti ba aiye je, Eko ki ise ilu Oyibo."-
Children of nowadays have spoilt the world. Lagos is not like London."

Eka ro ololufe mi-
Good morning my love

Ututuoma -
Good morning

Nna anyi-
Our father

"Eko oni baje"-
Lagos will not be despoiled

3.

ANNIHILATION

BY
CHIAGOZIE FRED NWONWU

Chapter 1

I
T TOOK MORE THAN THE SOUND OF THE ALARM built into the detachable chrome and fibreglass bed to wake Boyo up from sleep. Though the continuous beep of the alarm played a part, it was the strong, bittersweet, whiff of marijuana, seeping in through the hairline crack where his bulletproof fibreglass door failed to meet its thirty-year-old stainless steel metal frame. Like most things in his house, the door was bought second-hand from the Hausa traders that had made sales of second-hand items their preserve.

Lifting his head wearily from his synthetic feather pillows, he snapped his fingers twice to turn off the alarm, then tried to drift back to sleep.

The day was not a work day, for him at least, since he had put in the mandatory 48 hours work-week at the factory where he worked as a contract security guard. He was nudging again on dream world's door when the whiff of marijuana, stronger now, assailed his nostrils again. He coughed—a chest-wracking cough, which usually

73

pre-empted his asthma attack.

Sleep fled from him as he jumped out of bed and grabbed his inhaler, a sturdy transparent cone that glowed at his touch. He sucked on it for a few seconds then leaned back on the bed, waiting for the drug to take effect.

As soon as his chest stopped heaving, he pressed a small button on the bedside table and a compartment slid out. He rummaged inside and pulled out a small face mask, which he clamped on his face, covering his nose and mouth. He adjusted the mask to fit as snugly as possible and walked to the door.

Anger blazed in his eyes and his hands shook as he paused for a while behind the door, pondering if he should confront the perpetrators of this assault.

Deciding it had gone on long enough; he keyed in his clearance code with skill of long practice, looking away from the flashing neon pad, and waited for the heavy door to slide away, before stepping into the corridor.

He paused just outside the door and stared at the knot of half-nude youths, who ignored him as they passed around a gigantic joint of marijuana wrapped in what glowed like Syntogrip - which allowed the semi-legal drug burn more evenly and much longer than the conventional fibre wrapper.

Spent smoke clouded the passage, thick enough to get anyone that inhaled it high. Wanting to see the faces of the drugheads before he confronted them, Boyo snapped his fingers and the bluish light strips along the walls crackled and blinked to life, causing the roughnecks to exclaim with irritation even as they tried to shield their eyes—Syntogrip for sure, Boyo thought.

Syntogrip was usually soaked in TyrolineX - an illegal synthetic drug, popularly called TX, that a government survey said was responsible for more deaths the year before than the B viruses - explained why dealers got as much as twenty years for first offence and death for a repeat offence. TX was also very expensive. A 10-milligram bottle sells for as high as twenty thousand African Union Nirand - enough money to buy a house in highbrow Ejigbo or an entire street in swampy VGC. The going rate of TyrolineX was enough attraction for the multitude of criminal gangs that battled for control in the streets of Eko.

TyrolineX caused over-sensitivity to light, making it painful for the user to function in direct light. The default recourse for users was dark glasses. Its use among the rich and famous had recently spawned a new high fashion statement, shaded smart glasses that filtered out the harsher spectrums, which the group before Boyo were now hastily pulling down from forehead perches.

The mumbled curses coming from the group drew Boyo from his mental flight. Three males and two females barely out of adolescence, all heavily tattooed and sporting another recent craze, eye-side luminous tribal marking, occupied the space before the elevator. Boyo looked straight at the bigger of the two girls, a captivating young woman with colourful tiger tattoos and pointy breasts.

The nudity was another fashion craze that Boyo found difficult to understand. True, the climate had brought a lot of innovation to fashion, but nudity remained a taboo to the older generation across much of Africa. The younger generation, however, insisted on their right to go bare and flaunt their natural or acquired endowments.

The painted breast craze was made popular by a young female musician from the kingdom of Gambia, who appeared more often in just body paint than she did in clothes. Now, every girl younger than 25 was eager to throw clothes to the dustbin of ancient history and show off bare breasts decorated with tattoos and luminous tribal markings.

It took all of Boyo's self-restraint to keep his eyes from straying to the girl's firm post-adolescent breasts, highlighted by a clever use of body paint that made them appear to swell at any slight movement. He instead focused on the eagle tattoo that seemed to pulsate with life on her forehead.

"Tolani, I thought I had warned you several times about

smoking gbana in the passage?' He asked, trying to keep his voice clear despite the muffling effect of his mask.

She looked coolly at him - which was more than he hoped for; more often than not, she just ignored him - but said nothing. She took a long drag from the joint, just then passed to her, rolled the smoke in her mouth with seeming gratification and blew it towards him, managing somehow to do it in a sensual manner.

He could tell from the glassy sheen of her eyes that she was already too high to understand subtle cajoling, so he walked past her and her group, ignoring their giggles.

Cheeky tease, Boyo thought.

His intention was to call the landlord's attention to the nuisance that was his daughter and her disreputable friends. It was not that the burly local chieftain would have much to say, But Boyo wanted to air his grievance. However, their giggles got to him and he stopped short of ringing the buzzer over which his fingers hovered.

They stopped giggling when he turned away from the door and began walking towards them. Perhaps they retained enough reasoning in their drug induced high to read the anger in his eyes or perhaps it had more to do with Tolani, who had pushed herself to the front, nipples jabbing the air like darts.

Boyo quickened his stride as he neared them. Tolani seemed to guess his intent for she screamed obscenities at him and began sprinting forward.

Too late.

Her palm slammed on the cancel button less than a second after his palms had triggered the security alarm.

Everything happened in quick time after that.

Boyo gave Tolani credit for quick thinking. Aside from stopping for a moment to give him a killer gaze, with a speed Boyo was sure she derived from the TX, Tolani ushered her troop through the fire escape tube beside the elevator. She turned once more to glare at him, her eyes, dilated pupil and all, promising him repercussions, before sliding down the escape tube after them.

Chapter 2

Thirty minutes later, Boyo stood passive beside his door as the street magistrate examined his iris for signs of TX poisoning. She had already searched his apartment and her colleagues at that moment were searching the other apartments in the building.

She sighed and straightened up, peering at him, suspicious.

"Mr Boyo, there are still many loopholes in your story, true, the level of TX in your body could only have come from secondary smoke and will surely fade away in a few hours. And your asthma (she glanced at the mask now hanging from his belt) could not have tolerated any lengthy exposure to either form of TX, but there remains your claim that you have no knowledge of those responsible. For an event that happened just outside your quarters and for which you raised alarm, this leaves me with a lot of open questions." She said.

"But Magistrate Uche, I have already told you that I didn't see their faces. The corridor was unlit. Besides they jumped into the escape tube as soon as my door slid open." Boyo said, trying to sound as irritated as he could manage.

"You have said that before too," she reminded him, "but you are yet to tell me how someone at your pay level can afford a fibreglass security door?"

"You are only asking now. Clearly, you can see that it is second-hand. I bought it from the Hausa traders in old Idumota." He said, his irritation now was not feigned.

"So you say, but it could possibly be that you bought it new and now it is old." She allowed the smile lines around the corner of her eyes to let him in on her joke, but Boyo was already too infuriated to care much about her sense of humour.

"Anyway, she continued, "your security certificate says you are clean, so I have to take your word for it, but I still want you to come around the office later to view some gang tattoos which may help you identify the people responsible."

"I told you I didn't see much of them, how will I be able to describe tattoos that I have never seen?" Boyo asked.

"Mr Boyo, I take it you are not willing to cooperate. Do you want me to call your company and request a formal directive from them to make you comply? You know I can do that don't you?" she asked, her voice a little loud, for effect.

"Have it your way magistrate, I will still say the same thing I am saying now, and you'd be wasting your time."

"I don't think so Mr Boyo." She said, smiling coyly at him. "But like I said before, you are clean, so I will let this slide, but next time you smell TX in this area I will advise you alert us from your allincom, it wouldn't do to let drug heads know there is an alert out on them, would it?"

As she walked to the elevator, her team following her, she turned and gave him a slight wink, surreptitiously patting her breast pocket. Boyo did not react; he stood there scowling at her receding back until the elevator door closed behind her.

Boyo sighed as he entered his apartment. He hoped to avoid any encounter with his landlord who would at that moment be glued to the security scanner watching the magistrates depart.

As soon as the door slide closed behind him, Boyo thumbed the lock button and touched his breast pocket. He smiled as he withdrew a plastic card and looked at the florescent neon scrawl.

Magistrate Uche (Squad 2 Commander)
M Unit Headquarters,
State Secretariat,
Banana Island
Eko.

Chapter 3

Boyo felt the walls of his room too restrictive and decided a stroll through the soggy streets would clear his head. He knew he would need all his wits about him when he faced the magistrates later that day.

Strolling through the streets of Eko Island served as a kind of therapy for Boyo, he believed the sense of history that the old city evoked was balm to his numerous aches.

Some change called attention to themselves, like the buildings along the street in Obalende that Boyo was walking through.

On either side of the single lane street, there were still numbers of the four to five storey buildings that were in vogue some sixty years before. More numerous were the modern 10-15 storey pre-fabricated plastic and steel buildings.

Though some of the four and five storey structures retained enough of their original style to give a sense of antiquity, they all bore signs of restructuring. Boyo was sure that if the original builders were to see them, they would not recognise them.

It was not as if the present owners of the houses were redesigning for fun. The fact that most of these structures were built before the rise in sea level in 2030 swamped areas that had been well above sea level played a large part in the redesigning. Though much of the waters receded after about four years, the incident taught people to respect nature. Now people built houses with nature in mind, taking note of things like seismic patterns that though not ordinarily active in these parts had been known to occur - like the severe quakes that levelled Kumasi ten years before.

Most buildings had bases made of fibre glass coated steel rods that rose well above the highest recorded water line, with first floors usually uninhabited except for where some ingenious landlord had made it watertight enough to farm catfish or, as Boyo heard, a hybrid form of gbana that was said to grow well in salt water.

All around, the aluminium and plastic frames of solar panels glittered in the morning light. The panels themselves were black opaque squares that seemed to absorb the very air around their lofty perches. Boyo's eyes flickered uneasily to the roof of one of the newer buildings where a new generation hybrid cone, said to be a thousand times more efficient than the solar panels, pulsated with energy, glowing deep copper as it recycled watts of electric energy at the speed of thought.

Strange thing science, Boyo thought, someone invents something that absorbs energy and stores it for later use, another invents something else that not only absorbs that energy but also recycles it over and over.

He looked again at the cone. Wondrous! He knew the science behind it, had listened with rapt attention as his science teacher in secondary school explained how it worked, yet he found it difficult to understand how a single twenty-foot cone can reproduce enough energy to power twenty city blocks.

Even back then, the cone was a source of heated debate. Most students were quick to understand the economic implication of the cone, especially for a country that for years relied solely on income from petroleum-based products. That, perhaps, was responsible for some of the more outlandish arguments against the wide use of the cone.

Boyo was sure that these accusations, especially the one that claimed the cone was of devilish origins, were somewhat responsible for the snail-paced incursion of the technology into the country – not that the princely price that made it only affordable to governments and big corporations did much to help.

The cone he was looking at was one of the three that he knew of in the whole of Lagos, but he was sure that some rich people would have some others hidden away from prying eyes. Hiding the cone would not be a small task since it had the downside of requiring thousands of litres of water to cool its volatile core—another reason they are not in general use.

The honking of an amphibious scooter dragged him out of his musing and he jumped out of the pedestrian lane a few seconds before the scooter flashed past. The laughter of the three topless teens atop it floated behind them, reaching him after they had disappeared around the corner.

"Kids and the need for speed...," Boyo thought, as he straightened his light jacket and brushed off the specks of water that the scooter's exhaust had sprayed on his synthetic leather trousers, "yet the government complains about the cost of growing replacement body parts."

As he went past the facade of the building that hosted the cone, he quickened his pace, only slowing three blocks later. True, he had tried to curtail this instinctive fear of any building that housed a cone, but the event of five years earlier remained vivid in his subconscious. He was unfortunate to be in the vicinity where an experimental cone had exploded with great force after an apparently overworked water board staff had fallen asleep on duty, neglecting to reverse the water supply to the sector where the cone was located. The man had been asleep for not more than three minutes, enough time though, for the core to overheat and turn critical. Boyo escaped the blast because he was running after a felon who managed to escape in the general confusion. Since then, he always got that unconscious need to hurry past any cone installation and would only enter one if he had to.

Boyo slowed his pace as he neared the six-lane Awolowo Road and waited in line to use the automated pedestrian bridge that carried him across the expressway, there he waited in line to board the Bus Rapid Transit that will take him back home.

Chapter 4

Boyo encountered his landlord and his wife exiting the lifts on the ground floor as he walked towards the stairwell. He expected the wife to query him about the incident with the Magistrates but neither she nor her husband said anything about it. Though he considered the woman's disregard of his stammered greetings a sign of ill feeling, Boyo still managed the traditional half-prostration that was required of him.

His landlord seemed pleased enough with him, he even smiled as he patted Boyo on the back, ignoring his wife's scorching look.

Boyo hurried into the stairwell and ran all the way up to his fifth floor apartment. Though he was sure Tolani's parents were on their way out, he wanted to get to his room before the time it would take the lift to reach his floor. The woman may change her mind about going out and decide to talk to him about this morning's incident.

Ever since the visit from the magistrate, he had avoided any encounter with Tolani's parents. He knew that though they might play it down because he did not rat out on Tolani and her gang, they might still have a lot to say about him breaking protocol, not reporting the matter to his landlord before bringing the law into it.

It was at times like this that he rued what he had thought was a good decision, living on the same floor with the landlord and his family, granted that it did have its pecks in well-serviced facilities and prompt attention to complaints.

Nevertheless, it was not just because of them that he took the stairs.

He has what a psychoanalyst had called elevator phobia. Try as much as he did, he never could get used to that sudden drop that began a lift's movement, he always jerked with fear, and it took all his sanity to accept that the lift was not going to unhinge from whatever was holding it and plunge unfettered to the concrete floor below, with him in it.

At the landing, he heaved a sigh of relief when a brief glance towards the elevator screen on his floor showed no activity. Breathing deeply, he tried to control his racing heart as he approached his door.

He was sure that Tolani would react to his calling the magistrates on her, but he did not know what form it would take.

It was while he was keying his unlock code into his door that the whistle reached his keen ears. It was low enough for anyone else to ignore, meant for his ears only. Boyo ignored it at first, but the he heard his name, a harsh whisper, tinted with urgency. He turned towards the source and found Tolani, bare topside half out of her room - which was three doors down from his - beckoning him.

He did not want to go to her at first, but then a little smile played around the sides of her mouth and she made the pleading sign, rubbing her palms together in front of her. He shrugged and walked over to her.

He stopped in front of her, meaning to ask what she wanted but she did not give him the chance. As soon as he got within reach, she grabbed his shirt and pulled him into the room.

The door slid shut behind him and Boyo's heart skipped several beats as he heard the click of the auto lock sliding into place. He turned to her, alarmed, but she shushed whatever he meant to say with a kiss that probed the depth of his soul.

She latched on to his lips until he felt he would pass out from the sensation and lack of oxygen. Then she let go and drew back to look at him.

"That's for not ratting us out to the Magistrates," she said. He was still dazed when she pulled him close again, her lips seeking his in a mad dance that took him far away from the echoes of doubt on his mind, putting off the need to voice the questions that swirled in his head.

He had always desired crazy Tolani and though he was not sure about the propriety of his actions, the feel of her warm tongue probing the insides of his mouth and the sensation of those immaculate breasts pressing against his chest, were enough to cancel his doubts - at least for the moment.

When she released his lips and pulled him towards the bed, his mind still pondered the question of correctness but his body went willingly enough.

At the background, coming through a wall unit radio, he could hear a newscaster going on about a quake somewhere in the Atlantic Ocean. Though something told him it was important news, he could not focus his mind enough to process it, not with all that was happening to him.

Chapter 5

It was possibly the longest one hour of his life; he stood behind the door watching the offending boy in the holopane, wondering what magic he could perform to make him move, even if for a few seconds. He berated himself for not leaving when the urge to go nudged his mind, his inner man had told him to move then, but he was too engrossed with the thought of how much pleasure he could bestow on her.

Just a few moments before the nosy boy stepped into the passage, he had stood to go, but looking down at her succulent curves he had leaned towards her and what he thought would just be a brief kiss had deepened. They had slid to the floor, tearing off the few bits of garment they had managed to put back on in the interim.

It was then that the sound of his buzzer reached him, and the high-pitched voice began calling out his name. That was when it occurred to him that he had left his door unlocked. There would have been nothing strange in that if it was someone else's door, but he had garnered a reputation as a stickler to security detail, especially ensuring the security strip on his door was neutral green at all time. Boyo could not blame the kid, who obviously felt he had overlooked that aspect, especially in the light of recent happenings, and felt the need to inform him.

He regretted not buying that new all-in-one remote control app for his alincom. With that he would have locked the offending door from his present position, satisfying the kid and keeping his hard earned reputation.

The boy's continued ringing on his buzzer was already attracting attention. Boyo's heart skipped several beats when the voice of his landlord's wife, inquiring what the boy was doing, floated down from the elevator area. Apparently she and her husband had returned from their outing.

"Mama, it is Uncle Boyo's door. The security code is showing disengaged." The boy said, to the woman whose footsteps Boyo could hear clearly, as she drew closer to investigate, causing his heart to sink further.

"That is strange. Is Boyo in?" She inquired from the boy who was still busy pressing the buzzer, enjoying the sound it made, judging from the rhythmic way he was thumbing it.

"Yes ma, I saw him when he returned." The boy said, punctuating his statement with the buzzer.

"Maybe he has gone to the laundry, or is downstairs at Mama

Nneka's restaurant. Anyway, wait here for him, and stop ringing that buzzer. Tell him I want him to come take a look at my heat converter. It seems to have packed up."

Boyo was gratified with the sound of her receding footsteps, but his happiness faded quickly when he remembered he was stuck here, in her daughter's room, a place he was not supposed to be.

He felt the girl in question behind him even before her taut nipples pressed into the small of his back. He turned to look at her and was surprised at how unconcerned she seemed. Perhaps she was too high to understand the situation, but he doubted that. She had not had any fix since she pulled him into her room, and that was hours before.

She would have seized his lips again, had he not held her at bay.

"No," he said, shaking his head. "Your brother is out there."

Frowning slightly she looked at the holopane, turned back to him and asked

"What is he doing outside your apartment?"

"Apparently I forgot to re-lock my door." He turned to look at her, surprise colouring his voice, "you mean you did not hear all that went down before?"

She did not answer but tried to pull him back to the soft bed. He had a mind to follow her as the sight of her full buttocks heated up his blood, but the thought of what discovery would cost him, held him back. True, he had always desired Tolani. He had not acted on his desires for fear of her reaction, but she had initiated this. He believed it was to show gratitude for the way he handled the Magistrates. She had expected him to rat on her, when he did not, she began seeing him in a new light. Boyo had told himself not to read too much into it, as an addict, she must be well-versed in using sex as a tool.

He held back, unmoving, using his eyes to tell her no, not now. He watched, silent, as the light died in her eyes. She shrugged and went back to the bed, the coloured hairs of her pubic region reflecting the soft light that did little to brighten the room.

It took all his strength to draw his eyes away from her.

Outside, the boy had taken up position on an old crate opposite his room, waiting for him to return from wherever he went. He had stood behind the door, cursing his weakness, and praying for a miracle, something that will make the boy move before the other tenants returned

Looking back, he cursed himself for the carelessness that was about to cause him serious embarrassment.

Chapter 6

It took a while but Boyo at long last made up his mind to leave the room. Better the boy than the entire floor, he thought. Still baffled by Tolani's nonchalance, he stepped into the corridor. The door had opened on well-oiled wheels that cut to the barest minimum, any sound that would have attracted attention.

Boyo had waited until the boy's face was facing away from Tolani's door before stepping into the corridor, placing hope on mystery - yes, he would appear, the boy would see him, and be left guessing from where he appeared.

He crept onward, as silent as a spider and somehow managed to get about two feet from the boy, and probably eight feet from Tolani's room, when the boy turned, startled. The boy's mouth formed a big 'o' even as his chest seemed to pulsate with fear.

"Uncle Boyo," he said.

Chapter 7

Though Boyo had expected the boy to react to his sudden appearance, he did not bargain for the reaction he got. The boy seemed to get over his initial fear quick enough. He jumped up from his position on the crate, looked first at Boyo, who had stopped walking, then down the passage, then at Tolani's door, and back again at Boyo. He did this several times, his forehead furrowing as he tried to arrive at whatever conclusion his young mind was getting at. Then his big eyes opened wide, as if a light just went off behind them, but then the light died again as the boy discarded whatever

87

inspiration had struck him just then.

"Uncle Boyo," he began, "I have been waiting for you. Your security code is disengaged. You see I was right, I told mummy you are not in your room. But where are you coming from, the elevator is the other way?"

Boyo's heart lifted as the import of the Boy's summation hit him. What luck, he thought as he found his legs again. "Laundry," he offered, as he clicked the open button.

"Tolani was asking about you earlier," the boy said, following Boyo to his door. It had perhaps not occurred to him to ask about the clothes that Boyo went to launder.

"Was she?" Boyo said, wondering if he should send the boy away or just escape into his room before anyone else showed up. Instead, he rummaged inside his pocket and brought out two Five Nirand Chits, which he handed over to the boy only to watch it disappear into the boy's pocket within an instant. "I will see her later," he said to the retreating boy.

"Mummy wants you to check her heat converter, she said it's overheating," the boy said before he jumped into the escape chute.

Boyo sighed and entered his room, not believing his luck. As he crossed over to the cold box for a pack of water, he noticed that his body was drenched in sweat. Nothing that a shower won't fix.

"I will never take this kind of risk again," he thought as he walked towards the shower unit. He looked back at the sensuality of his time with Tolani and questioned himself again on the propriety of sleeping with his landlord's daughter and the consequence of it getting out.

He tried to shake his mind off it as the plastic walls of the shower unit enclosed him.

The warm water from the shower cascaded down his face before running in rivulets down his body to disappear into the drain on a journey that would lead it to millions of other showers in the state and perhaps, back to this one, after being purified at the treatment plant.

The touch of a raised knob changed the temperature of the

water to icy cold, then to almost scalding hot before the sound of a beep warned him he was fast nearing the standard water ration.

He leaned towards the wall, covered with recycled plastic tiles, and thumbed off the supply switch, wondering for the thousandth time how a city-state surrounded by water would resort to rationing. He knew this recent rationing was because of the apparent contamination of the 70% of the fresh water supply by a steadily rising sea level, which was continuously pushing the coast further inland every other rainy season. Even though he had heard the explanations of the water resource people - who wanted everyone to believe that the state was doing everything possible to battle the prevailing water crisis - he still felt they were not doing enough, especially where more efficient water treatment technologies were concerned.

He sighed as the shower hose retracted into the wall and hot air whirled around him, drying his damp body within a short time. Wanting to extend his bliss for as long as possible, he walked to his antique mirror, the only inheritance he got from his mother - who assured him it was an authentic Chinacraft purchased in Dubai between 2002 and 2004; the mirror was not of the best quality, even for 2002. Yet it remained a collectors item due to its origins.the notoriety of its producer country then made it a collectible - something that was helped by t he fact that it wore poorly and took serious effort to maintain.

Boyo gazed at his slightly elongated profile. Even though, he could not be considered truly handsome, he was still striking enough to turn heads, with bulging muscles that threatened to rip through his fitted clothes and all. His full lips and upward slanting eyes gave him a friendly expression that drew people to him.

A little short of six feet, Boyo had learnt over the years to walk straight and this made him appear taller.

Boyo smiled as he contemplated what the magistrate's gesture meant. He knew she did not really need him to identify the culprits and since he was not responsible for their action in any way, he was not required to undergo any truth searching. That left only one option, something that her wink clearly spelt out: she wanted him for something altogether private.

Boyo wondered what she saw in him. Magistrate Uche was not a stranger to him, since his security circuit was under the jurisdiction of her command their paths had crossed, but this was the first time their meeting would be because of something that pertained to him. In their previous meetings, he was either reporting a crime or handing over criminals he had arrested on the job.

His job as a private security officer ensured he got almost the same sort of training as the magistrates and he, like them, was allowed to carry firearms, though only when he was on duty. Unlike the magistrates though, he was not allowed to dispense justice on the spot and had to handover anyone he arrests on duty to the nearest M-Unit: the Magistrate Unit.

The magistrates, popularly called Magis, are a unit of the police force formed to fight the drug lords who once controlled the country's economy - everything from banks, hotels, hospitals and even had substantial stakes in the major energy companies.

Back when the drug lords held sway, an enterprising Indian scientist had just invented TyrolineX, which started out as a cancer cure. Though the scientist had known about the drug's soon-to-be notorious side effect, he had reasoned that the long-term benefits far outweighed its addictive property. He hoped that further research would help cut down on the psychosomatic side effect and make the drug less addictive. He did not reckon with the Chinese counterfeiters, who successfully cloned TyrolineX within the first year and isolated its addictive psychosomatic properties a few weeks after their counterfeit drug went on sale. Before the end of the second year, they had turned TyrolineX into a much sought-after high fashion drug. By this time, the non-addictive version was already on sale, albeit at a much cheaper price than its derivative. While governments were spending billions trying to refine the drug and remove its addictive and hallucinogenic properties, the drug lords were spending more trying to extract just the opposite, though the official researchers succeeded first, the drug dealers were right on their heels.

Because of the infiltration of the security agencies by the drug lords, who paid huge sums to secure freedom for apprehended traffickers, the government created the magistrates—an order of handpicked security officers known for their zeal and willingness to break the circle of crime. The magistrates were so-called because they were empowered by law to try cases at the scene of the crime without recourse to the courts.

The melodious chime of the digital clock broke Boyo's mental flight, but not before he had pondered the sense, in naming a cancer drug after a now disused paint base said to be a cancer causative agent. Strange name choice.

He tied a loose towel around his torso and stepped into his room, still undecided whether to take up the beautiful law officer's offer.

Chapter 8

The digital hour hand of the big clock tower near the marina had already crawled past mid-day and was heading towards the second hour after noon when Boyo walked through the harbour to take a boat taxi to Banana Island.

Luckily for him, it was still way before rush hour, which would have seen the waterway choked with boat taxis and the more numerous personal boats ferrying workers to and from the government secretariat on Banana Island.

Boyo peered over the side as the boat crossed the yellow buoy that marked the former shoreline. Through the brackish water, he could see the black and white kerbs and the still perfect looking interlocking stones on roads that were now underwater.

Boyo wondered how nature preserves some things while breaking others down into their constituent elements.

The thought of old roads and their durability reminded him of the long abandoned bridge that still presents a massive presence on the other side of what used to be a lagoon. The Third Mainland

Bridge still stood, even if disused, as a testament to the prowess of the German builders who left their mark across the nation. Beside it, like a mockery of the simplistic nature of the past, lay the ever lengthening construct that the new city state administrators called Sixth Mainland Bridge and Business Hub.

Boyo had never liked that construction, which he saw as a flagrant abuse of wealth and authority, a bid by an administration to lay claim to a legacy. Boyo hissed. Like many of the inhabitants of the Eko City-State, Boyo had little love for the city's young administrator, who swept into office on the strength of his grandfather's name.

In Boyo's opinion, the massive, money guzzling length of the sixth mainland bridge attests to the fact that Bankole Tinibu would bankrupt the state pretty soon if he continues spending public funds the way he is doing.

The boat slid through the water, following the submerged road that led straight to a pier, its shadow startling shoals of brightly coloured fish that sought refuge in even-spaced holes, which used to hold neon lights, now rutted away, leaving strips of plastic held down by rusty screws.

The boat bumped into the pier and he looked up from the water just in time to see the automatic locks on the boats bow clinch into the rubber and plastic moorings, holding the boat fast.

He waited for the other passengers to alight. He had always hated that sudden need for people to get off seats they had fought for at the other side. If someone could sit still for minutes while crossing the lagoon, what was so hard in waiting a few seconds for the people ahead to alight? Well, he was not that impatient so he avoided all the pushing and shoving. He was not the only one with that thought today, as two passengers, a man and a woman, also waited for the ramp to clear.

Soon enough the passengers had all alighted, then he made his way across the ramp.

He had just stepped onto the pier and was taking in its

plastic expanse when he overheard the captain of the boat he arrived on complaining to another in the next boat about the strange tide pattern that day.

"Wole, I don dey this place for years now, but I have never seen a tide as low as we had this morning." the captain said, a tinge of what appeared to be fear in his voice.

"Yes Fabien," Wole replied, "My brother had to battle to move his boat into the water this morning. na tugboat dem take pull am from sand. Though it was late when he left, he has already returned and is at home now, he caught more than a week's catch within a few hours."

"Wow," Fabien exclaimed. "A week's catch, that's big. I say it's a good omen, abi?"

"Yes it is a very good one, whatever made the tides low must have caused the fish to move towards land," Wole said, smiling broadly "and my brother said it was the calmest sea he had seen in a long time." He added as he unsnapped his boat from its clasp in readiness for the journey across the lagoon.

Captain Wole's boat surged away with a brief spurt of his engine, his friendly wave to Fabien was returned with equal gusto.

Something in their conversation, something he could not quite place, caused Boyo to glance again at the shoreline, where waves lapped the beach of the artificial island. As far as he could tell, the water was as high as it had ever been. Perhaps because the tide was in again, he thought. Shrugging, he turned to continue to his destination.

Before him loomed the twelve storey Ocean Parade Towers, home to a multitude of government agencies including the Magistrates Unit Headquarters. The Ocean Parade Towers was one of the few buildings that survived the demolition hammer after a government survey deemed most of the partially submerged buildings on Banana Island to be 'disasters-in-waiting'.

The Ocean Parade Towers was spared because its developers made allowance for foreseeable natural disasters. All the same, the government had deemed it prudent to build a concrete moat, complete with sluice gates and automatic surge controls, around it—something that was replicated more or less around other buildings on the artificial Island, giving the buildings a nest-like look that had become so popular it was being adopted by many.

The government, bowing to the pressure from Big Business, gave up its land holding in Ikeja and moved its administrative headquarters to Banana Island which was then largely uninhabited. Now the island bustled with people on government business or visiting relatives in the maximum-security prison on the other side of the island.

Boyo ignored the touts outside the building who were flashing various government documents as they tried to get him to patronise them. Whispers of 'affidavit' and 'citizen stamp' floated from even the most unusual sources. Though the government had tried to put a stop to touting in the secretariat, the efforts were half-baked as people argued that the touts were more of an assert than an inconvenience, since they helped those who lacked the time to spare to procure documents that would have taken hours in just a few minutes.

His security clearance got him as far as the inner recess of block 'A' where a mild mannered, smartly dressed junior magistrate, behind a bulletproof screen asked again for his security clearance and which department he was visiting before pointing him towards a long well-lit passage that led to a stairwell and banks of lifts.

He would have naturally taken the stairs, even though he was headed ten floors up, and was already headed that way when another cool-looking magis stepped in front of him. Though she had on the in-house uniform of blue-black suit, the silver eagle on her lapel marked her as a para-combatant, as did the well-worn quality of the grip of the pistol that hung low from her waist.

"Are you Mr Boyo... here to see Magistrate Uche?" She inquired, her voice telling him that she already knew who he was and the question was just a formality.

"Well well," Boyo thought, "a big bird to receive me,

somebody must want me to breeze past security."

"I am Boyo," he answered, not bothering to answer the second question.

"Magistrate Uche is waiting for you in her office." She said, ushering him towards one of the lifts.

Boyo steeled himself and followed her into the transparent lift.

As the elevator slid to a halt on the tenth floor, Boyo braced himself for the coming jolt. Much to his embarrassment, the woman seemed to sense his distress as he jerked suddenly and instinctively reached out for the elevator wall. Then, the door slid open and the smiling magistrate stepped out signalling for him to follow.

Chapter 9

The magistrate led him through a large room occupied mainly by banks of high-tech computers and their human operators, most wearing the large goggles and headsets that allowed them interact with the computers.

Their movements would have been quite theatrical if Boyo did not know that they were operating in cyber world, handling mind-boggling tasks that were so secret, only the operator could see what it was. Still he allowed a small smile as he watched the break dance-like movement of one of the agents.

Magistrate Uche's office was at the end of the large hall, beyond the desks and computers. The magistrate led him to the door and turned smartly to walk back the way they came. Boyo was not given any chance to collect his thoughts as the door swung open and Magistrate Uche stood there looking directly at him, a small smile playing at the corners of her lips.

She held the door open for him as he crossed into the large office. It was a swing door. They were making a comeback, though Boyo was sure hers, like most in this building, came with the house - 60-70 year antiques that he was sure would fetch a handsome fee at the antique market. She did not go round the glass desk but perched on the edge directly opposite him, her smile was deeper now and she appeared amused by something that was lost to him.

"So you decided to come?" She asked, still smiling.

"Yes, I thought it would be better to avoid any problems at work." He said, not hiding his sarcasm.

"Boyo, let's cut to the chase ok, I did not call you here to just look at gang tattoos," she looked more serious now. "We have looked up your security file and have come to an understanding that your present job is way below your qualification and experience."

"What are you talking about?" Boyo asked, confused.

"Well, I recommended you for reserve duty with the Magistrates, don't worry; it was well before today's events." She said, looking serious.

Magistrate Uche's words astounded Boyo. Reserve duty with the magis meant almost ten times his present salary and the chance of being elevated to full magistrate after five months if he performed satisfactorily. He wanted so much to be elated but he was sure that he had heard somewhere that the magis do not give out boons; there will be payment ahead if he takes this offer, perhaps of a kind he would rue.

"What is the catch?" he asked, looking her in the eye.

"I see you assume there would be one?" she said.

"Isn't there always?"

"Well, there isn't in this case, you were already pencilled down for reserve duty. But as it is, we won't mind you looking into the source of the TX that we found in the discarded Syntogrip on your floor as a first case." She said, still smiling.

Boyo looked at her warily, wondering why she was placing her cards so simply on the table. "And you said there was no catch." He said.

"I don't see one, as magistrates, it is our duty to investigate crime, or do you know more about this than you are letting out?" suspicion played for a moment in her eyes.

"No... no," He stammered, "I just thought that a minor case..."

"You thought wrong. The magistrates don't close cases

unless they are solved beyond all reasonable doubt; as such we are not done with that case. The thing is, we have been trying to get a break on the island TX market and believe me, if we can get a single retailer, he or she could be the link to the dealers we have been waiting for." Her eye narrowed to slits as she looked closely at him, as if to read his mind, "but the question remains, do you want to come in or not, because all these speeches would be unnecessary if you do not."

"I have always wanted to be a Magistrate." Boyo said, wondering how to get round to interrogating Tolani, especially after what happened between them earlier that day.

"And you now have that chance. I saw your four previous applications, so I know this offer is not one you can easily refuse."

"Yes," Boyo began, looking her square in the face, "That is the thing, four applications, all turned down, now this, if I was not good enough to get in then, why now, especially out of the blues?"

"It is not exactly out of the blues. There is usually a long waiting list of qualified candidates from all over the country. To get in, you have to either be exceptionally gifted or get recommendations from four group heads. Moreover, those recommendations come after serious evaluations. You couldn't get in before because you already had three recommendations for your very first application; your subsequent applications were not even considered because you had already advanced beyond the application process."

Boyo did not realise that his jaw was hanging open until she indicated that by touching her lower jaw with her palm and acted like she was pushing it closed. Embarrassed, he quickly closed his mouth. "I don't believe this. You mean all these years it only needed one signature to get me called up?"

"But that is only the half of it; you actually did get called up."

"What do you mean I actually got called up? I never got any notification to that effect and I sure didn't change my email."

"Well, let's just say we make sure our prospective candidates stay that way. That is why we arranged for you to work for Harrier Security, where you received the same training a

Magistrate cadet gets. Truth is, Harrier Security seconds as a training school." Boyo was too surprised to say anything; he just sat there looking incredulously at the woman who he had thought had wanted to see him for something altogether private. Yeah right, if she looked like she was coming on to him then; she sure looked like someone he couldn't touch with a ten-foot pole now—without getting burned that was.

"So you see, you were already working for us, you just didn't know it." She said.

Boyo made his way down the stairs, enjoying the solid feel of his boots on the rungs. Left to his own device he had decided against using the lift and had detoured into the stairwell as soon as Magistrate Uche said goodbye and returned to her office.

Boyo had since come to terms with his phobia and felt no pang of shame for his apparent cowardice, though in this case his decision had more to do with wanting to clear the cotton wools that seemed to be clouding his mind.

Then there was the question of his new status. He accepted the offer. Well, it was not as if he had any choice, the job was actually a life changing one and highly sought after. The pay was good, actually too good, for the government wanted to make it very difficult to bribe the magis.

Acceptance was easy for him because the job was one he had sought. Though the issue of Tolani and her gang bugged his mind still, he knew how important it was to win the battle against the drug lords, but he was not fully convinced it would be any big break arresting Tolani and her gang. He felt sure they were just recreational drug users, who did not know the implication of what addiction to TX would do. "How do they afford TX?" He pondered, "that stuff is not cheap."

The magistrates must think he knew more about the case than he was letting on, but he could not fathom why they would think so. He again rued hitting that alert button. Why had he not kept his temper in check? Why had he put the wheels of fate into motion? He shrugged away his ill feelings, as he reached the ground floor, still unable to find answers to his many questions.

Chapter 10

Boyo jumped out of the boat before it had even settled into the automatic mooring, and was already hurrying down the plastic pier towards the marina before any of his fellow passengers alighted.

He had grown to hate the springy feel of the bolted plastic beams that make up the pier. The bouncy feeling reminded him too much of the other purpose of the pier, buoyancy support. The government had decided that preparing for the rainy day also included adding as much buoyancy as possible to the structures around the seashore, that way, they reasoned, more lives would be saved if the sea rose unexpectedly again.

The plastic pier did reassure many people but for Boyo, it was too much of a reminder of the dangers of living in a coastal city. He hurried across, rushing to get his legs on solid ground and stop the queasiness that was threatening to push the contents of his stomach out of his mouth.

It was dusk; and the horizon echoed the fading rays of the sun. Ordinarily, he would have stayed to watch the shifting colours around the horizon, not now though. Shifting emotions battered his mind. As soon as he gave in to the feeling of happiness that came from his new status, the other thing, quite related to that status, crept up and threw a pall over his mood.

"Perhaps I should turn down the job," he thought as he walked slowly along the old marina route, his legs kicking up puffs of fluffy white sand that sparkled faintly under the streetlights that had just come on. However, that would mean giving up on my dreams and all for one lay in the sack with a temptress. He shook his head slightly, knowing even then that he was lying to himself, she was more than just a one-off lay. While her kiss pressed on his lips earlier that day, he had felt more than just the usual stirring. "Yes, there is more there," he thought.

It was then that a thought struck him, a solution to all his problems. Yes, it should be easy. "Get her to tell me who her supplier is and forward the information to the Magistrates, perhaps even get her to register for the legal government-issued substitute for Tyroline which should help her control her urges for the drug, yes that is the solution."

His head cleared as those thoughts rushed through his mind; he was even beginning to smile. That was when he heard the sound. He stopped walking and turned towards the Atlantic Ocean. His heart almost stopped when he recognised the sound for what they were, alarm bells.

Wild eyed, he looked around in panic and noticed that people were running away from the seaside, abandoning cars and scooters, some heading towards the skyscrapers around the marina while many others just ran helter-skelter, screaming.

Boyo stared at the nearest bell pole a few metres away in the sea; it vibrated with the buzzing of the alert bell on its head, the warning light around the bell flashing red in the gathering dusk. It was only then that he noticed that the sea had receded drastically enough to show several metres below the watermarks of the derelict ships nearby.

Fighting rising panic, he turned once again towards the old marina, littered with abandoned cars and personal effects, past the running people, gauging his options.

Deciding salvation lay more towards the pier and its safety harnesses than in trying to make it to the old skyscrapers in the distance, Boyo took off with haste even as the warning bells tolled critical, changing tones faster than the emergency drills had suggested they would. "Then it must be very big, bigger than any ever recorded here and moving very fast," Boyo thought, glancing briefly at the calm sea, whose only remarkable difference was the lack of waves and the larger than usual stretch of beach.

Then he saw it, first through the corner of his eyes, a slight movement. He turned fully and the sheer beauty of it stayed his feet.

It was several storeys high and growing. Its movement was barely noticeable as it appeared to be stationary with only the increase in height betraying that, and just barely.

Boyo stood there staring in disbelief until the sound of one of the derelicts getting overwhelmed reminded him of his peril. He turned once again and ran for the pier where he could see several people struggling to strap in.

"Surely, there must have been some sort of warning," he thought. "If there was, how could I have missed any announcements to this effect?"

It was very close now. Boyo didn't have to look to know that, the noise reaching his ears told him all he needed to know. Though he was tempted to look, he forced himself to focus on the pier that was then just a few metres away, praying he not just reached it in time but that he got to strap in too.

He was about to believe reaching the pier impossible when the mottled green plastic loomed in front of him. Exhausted, he dived for the nearest strap-on. He barely had time to strap on his face mask that hung limp from its usual place on his belt and with great haste buckle the nearest strap-on he could reach around his torso before the first waves hit.

Hope of surviving the worst of the tsunami was playing through his head when he felt a sharp knock on his head as a piece of the broken derelict rammed into him. Somewhere, far of, the thought of a girl with tattooed breast and a drug habit flashed across his mind.

The last thing he saw as the lights went out of his eyes was the manufacturing date and model number of his facemask-'astmask 2® 20-05-2059'-as it floated by, snagged by the same piece of metal that had struck him.

Chapter 11

Boyo came to amidst debris and seawater. He tried to open his eyes, but a searing pain that appeared to come from behind his eyes made him winch and decide to keep his eyes shut in the mean time.

After a while, he tried opening his eyes again and though the throbbing pain persisted, he was slowly able force his eyes to obey by opening them an inch at a time.

There was chaos all around him. People were either struggling to get out of their harnesses or helping others do the same. After several attempts, Boyo managed to unbuckle his harness and stood up groggily to his feet. It was then that he understood that he was no longer at the pier. Yes, he was still on the pier, but the plastic and fibreglass construct had functioned as its builder has envisaged. The pier, unhinged from its mooring by the surging waves, had floated and carried its occupants further inland and deposited them several metres from where the pier had been when the water subsided. A spider silk rope, running from the bottom of the pier to the mooring made sure they did not go any further.

There were wounded people on the pier and a quick look around revealed devastated buildings as the cries of the injured pervaded the evening air.

The water had not fully subsided and Boyo could tell that it was still several metres above sea level, but it had lost the force with which it had struck. Boyo tried not to think about the fatalities that would have resulted from this tsunami, knowing that the suddenness with which it happened would have caught many people unawares.

Looking away from the image of a derelict embedded into the fourth floor of a skyscraper and several cars floating belly up in the seawater, Boyo focused on his immediate surrounding and called up his knowledge of first aid as he moved to help a middle-aged woman who had a nasty looking gash on her forehead. Using his shirt sleeve as bandage, Boyo tried to ignore the faint throbbing behind his head and concentrated on tying the makeshift bandage as tightly as he could.

He had finished dressing up the woman and was working on his fifth patient, a young man with a broken arm, when his allincom beeped.

He had the mind to ignore the call, but the tone sounded urgent. He pulled out the device, which thankfully was water-resistant, and thumbed the answer button.

It took him a while to recognise the face that stared at him from the screen, but soon recognised her to be the officer that had escorted him to Magistrate Uche's office a few hours before.

"What is your status Magistrate Boyo?" She asked, looking officious and serious.

"I am okay, found safety on the pier harness, we have some casualties here. I am currently giving first aid to the wounded." Then it struck him, she had called him magistrate, he marveled at her ability to engage in sarcasm amidst the chaos he knew the security service must be in now. "And I am not a magistrate, yet." He added. He kept his voice cold, trying let her know he did not appreciate her sarcasm.

"Believe me Boyo, you're officially a magistrate, at least until this mess is cleared up. All cadet reserves were called up to active service ten minutes ago. However, your third recommendation went up approximately two hours ago, that's how long you have been a full-fledged magistrate. You should have the official notification on your allincom." She was looking at him sourly.

Boyo looked at the mail marker on the left side of his allincom and found the green official seal indicating a government mail blinking. Knowing it must have come when he was unconscious, he could only manage to indicate comprehension when the officer informed him that an amphibious vehicle already has his location and would pick him and some of the wounded in two minutes.

He read the long document, skipping whole pages until he got to the part that required his thumb print. He pressed his right thumb print on the marker, instantly sending his acquiescence to the security database. He received a reply immediately, a congratulatory message from the security computer network and his barge number and security pass to a locker in M Unit that contained his uniforms and other tools of the trade. Though he had not expected anything less from an organised force such as the magis, he still found that he was quite impressed that even at a time of disaster such as this; things still functioned at one hundred percent.

With the weight of new responsibilities at the fulfilment of a childhood dream, Boyo turned his mind once more to the injured young man, whose wide eyes showed he heard much of Boyo's conversation. He was almost done splinting the injured man's arm when the amphibious vehicle pulled up beside the pier.

As Boyo walked towards the vehicle, his mind once again touched on the matter of the TX and the girl Tolani. Though he was sure more important matters had overtaken the matter for now, in the future, the case would be revisited and would become his assignment.

"Would there still be need for investigations now?" He wondered.

Before the extent of the tsunami's impact overwhelmed him again, Boyo wondered if he would ever find the willpower to resist Tolani, for even now, he remained unsure of his feeling towards her, but he knew he would not bear to see her in jail. If she survived this, he thought, looking out from the window of the amphibious vehicle at what were surely bodies floating in the receding seawater.

4.

A STARLIT NIGHT

BY

KOFO AKIB

1

EVERYBODY WAS SEATED around the oval-shaped conference table, except Stan. He entered the room shortly and tried to appear unnerved. He first readjusted his tie, and then fixed his faux smile, as a bale of repulse welled in his stomach. He muttered his apology and quietly found a vacant seat at a far corner. The same familiar ache that had plagued his heart for a long time returned and he yearned to stroll out of the room and never return. But he had to keep earning to keep Simbi. It sounded like a rule. It was.

When he saw that attention had been diverted from him, he brought out his cell phone and punched the *MyView* button. Instantly, Simbi's apartment flashed on his screen. Her living room was empty, so he navigated to the bedroom. She wasn't there. He moved to the kitchen, and there she was, moving about in her agbada-ish flowing gown, preparing a meal of what-he-could-not-see. He felt a surge of love and his heart skipped.

Stan knew the head of his department was retiring. He knew

he was qualified to take his place. But he also knew he wasn't going to get it. The politics here stinks, I can never be a good player. So he braced himself for the bitterness that was to come and gave his mind the permission to be any where but there.

"Good morning ladies and gentlemen," Mr. Njoku, the President of the Media conglomerate boomed.
Stan looked up in time to mouth the "Good morning sir" with the rest of the Staff.

Mr. Njoku noisily cleared his throat and said "this is not going to take long; we are going to have reports from various departments, and present the award for the staff of the year 2060."

Who could she be talking to? Stan thought absorbed in the drama unfolding on his cell. Simbi was no longer in the kitchen. She was now sitting on the edge of her bed, chatting excitedly with someone on her cell. All of a sudden, she stood up and raced out of the room. What? What happened?

"……. the company this year has recorded a staggering increase in clientele base…"
He heard cheers and applause and automatically joined. He looked up and saw that the head of his department was delivering a speech. His last speech. No! Stan quickly wrenched the weak hope that took root on his mind, before it grew into something he couldn't control.

"….I've had a remarkable time working with you all. But, there is always a time like this. I hope whoever succeeds me would take this section unto a greater height….." God, maybe it was a bad idea after all to connect his *MyView* to her apartment. When Stan first learnt about the new mobile technology, he openly criticised it, and made sure Simbi had the impression he was one of the people against the technology. Then he had discreetly fixed the magnetic microchip in her living room, bedroom and kitchen. He knew Simbi wouldn't have suspected. He always felt this compulsion to know what she did every minute, so the advent of the *MyView* technology was a mighty solution. Or was it? But why did she run from the room like that? Is somebody at the door? Who?

He knew he should at least, appear to be a part of the meeting, but he had to check this last time. So he stealthily brought his phone below the edge of the conference table, so that he could watch the screen and still appear to be checking his note on the table. Good! He swiftly went back to the living room. Nothing. Nobody. He navigated to the toilet; of course, no signal. So he went back to the kitchen and there she was throwing all the windows wide open. What? Smoke! Stan panicked, but then he saw Simbi carry a pot of what-he-could-not-tell to the sink. Oh! The food got burnt, again.

"...the best staff of the year is the same the man that would now head the client service department. His track record has ...."

"Simbs, when it comes to burning food, you deserve an award!" Stan was amused. He wondered why he never minded her clumsiness. He was sure she could still put something delicious together.

"... And the award goes to..."

Simbi...
Silence...

Stan felt all the eyes in the room focused on him.
"What?" he asked the excited woman by his side.
"You have just been named the staff of the year." The woman gawked at him. "You are the new head of the client service department."
"Mr. Bamiwo?"
"Of course... of course... Yes. I am too stunned, I can hardly believe this." He stood up, "thank you, thank you," he said, too surprised, and found his way around the giant oval conference table to receive the award. Cameras flickered as he reached for the award.

Stan felt honoured, happy and sad, he was so grateful yet he felt so ungrateful. He never expected this. He had always blamed the system; he never knew he was appreciated. With an invisible hand, he reached for his treacherous soul and squeezed out the bile juice. He had been so wrapped up in selfish desires he never took the time to appreciate what he had.

He looked up at the beaming faces and he felt overwhelmed. "I feel very happy and honoured and I appreciate all of you for this; everyone who has been a part of me. I have learnt from you all, and what I took away has made me worthy. I have lived beyond the day I thought it would all end to see this day. I owe it all to you. Thank you for making me the custodian of this..." He raised the award and everybody cheered loudly.

Mr. Njoku took his hand again and shook it firmly, "we are all very proud of you and we have entrusted this new responsibility to you because we know you will do just fine. Congratulations."
Stan was beyond himself with excitement, he couldn't wait to get to Simbi.

Everything was going to be okay.

2

Abigail, a new ward attendant at the Lagos metropolitan clinic, looked at the man lying on the bed, she was puzzled.
Something about this man seems so ridiculously familiar. Like he belonged to a life she was yet to live. The life she had been waiting for. She knew she mustn't be caught doing this, but this moment was very important. Her business was to clean the room and change the sheets. She has been doing that for the last two months. Entering this room and looking at this unconscious man had always been the best part of her day.

What could be so enchanting about a man in coma who cannot even see the face she had come to lightly powder whenever she was coming to see him, or smell the soft perfume she had never cared for, not in a very long time, but now wore. What kind of a woman would walk out on a man like this? She had heard things during the short time she had been here. Her colleagues had cursed Stan's fiancée in every language known to them. She was a sophisticated actress who sucked the man dry and left him when he lost his job.

Abigail gently traced a finger from his forehead down to the ridge of his nose and delicately lingered on his lips.

' Stan ' she breathed 'I want to be here when you wake up , you have been gone for so long, and when you finally open your eyes, you need to behold a beautiful sight , you need to smell love, feel love. I know I am not wrong, because I have known you deeply for a very long time, we just haven't met.'

The door opened and Aduke Bamiwo and Dr. Fernandez walked in. Abigail quickly pretended to be tucking the sheets. She turned briskly and greeted the intruders.

'Good morning Doctor Fernandez, good morning Mrs. Bamiwo.'

'Morning lady 'the doctor said and went to examine Stan.
Aduke approached Abigail. She froze not knowing what the older woman was about to do. Damp sweat broke on her brow as she felt Aduke place a hand on her shoulder.

'Thank you for taking good care of my son' she looked around her, the room was clean. 'I have noticed so many changes since you came around. You take care of your patients with so much love and care.'

'Thank you ma'am ... I really enjoy doing this,' Abigail blushed.

'I think you have a heart for this job and ...'

'Abigail, you are still in this room?' Aduke was cut short as the door was suddenly flung open and the matron angrily pushed her bulk inside. 'You spend all day doing nothing but God-knows-what in this room while other rooms reek with dirt,' she screamed.

'No, no .... no matron, I am done.. I was about leaving.'

'Ah...ah,' Aduke gasped in disbelief.

'Get out, and go clean the other rooms,' the matron commanded.

Abigail hurried out of the room, embarrassed.

'Sorry Madam. Please, don't mind that. How is he doing?' the matron said apologetically.

'Ehm ... He ... He is fine. I hope.'

'Don't worry, he will soon come around. We have seen cases like this before and they usually come around,' the matron said.

"Thank you matron."

"It's alright." The matron said and left the room. Aduke went to talk to the doctor.

"Doctor it's been five months, will he ever come round? Will he... will he be normal, sane again?" Aduke asked.

"Perfectly," the doctor said. "Mrs. Bamiwo, the last brain scan we did confirmed that your son had sustained no trauma to the brain," the doctor told her.

"Oh thank God. Then why is he still unconscious?"

"We initially pegged it on shock but after the last blood test we began to query a different cause."

"What cause?"

"Time travelling."

"What?"

"Yes," the doctor continued "the blood test revealed the presence of a substance in his blood stream."

"What, what substance.... Tell me, was he doing drugs?"

"No, Madam, calm down. You see, this substance once in the blood stream can dissociate the human body from the seat of consciousness. When this dissociation occurs, an individual's consciousness can travel at a speed faster than light."

"I don't understand any of this."

"Listen, let me explain. Anybody capable of moving faster than light can manipulate the space-time continuum, even an intangible body like human consciousness. This means he can travel to the future and the past. We are positive your son has time-travelled. The use of the substance is still one of a kind in time travel.

The transportation is not bodily, the traveller holds the destination in mind, and in less than three minutes after injecting the substance, he gets transported while the body remains."

"Oh my God, what do we do? How do we get him back?" Aduke sobbed.

"Madam, this is the most dangerous mode of time transportation. The body must be kept intact for the return to be possible, if he sustains an injury that alters the form in which he left his body, he might not be able to make the return."

"And he took the injection shortly after he ran into a moving van?" Aduke was alarmed.

"Yes, it makes sense now; he was trying to destroy his body so that return would not be possible. He intended to live on in a new world; whether in the past or future is what we cannot tell. Do you have any idea why he may do that?"

"He lost his job. He was actually expecting to be promoted, and then, he didn't get it. Then he said things in annoyance. He got fired and the woman he was about to marry left him."

"My humble guess is that he is trying to re-live all the dissatisfying experiences he had here. I bet he is either in the future or the past getting promoted and taking his bride to the altar. Or, are there other reasons why you think he might have done this?"

'Doctor, that is as much as I know. Help me, what can we do?''

"Two things," Dr. Fernandez shook two fingers in the air.

"We either wait for him to make his return. In that case, he will just wake up as if from sleep."

"Or?" Aduke urged.

'We slowly withdraw his contaminated blood and replace it with new blood. Once the substance is out of his body, he fades away from wherever he is and wakes up in the present. This process however may cause some damage to the brain because of the substance still present in his blood stream. He will still be able to function in every way, except that he will no longer have any strong emotions."

'Oh, oh, please doctor, there must be another way out ... no, please," Aduke turned to looked at Stan's sleeping form, then she began to rain blows on him in hysteria. "Why, why, why?" She pounded harder and shook the bed vigorously. "You wicked, heartless son. How could you do this to me?" she screamed. She sobbed.

"Stop. Stop that this instant," the doctor cautioned.

"No," Aduke screamed back.

"You want to kill him? The body has to be pres..." the doctor tried to explain

"Yes, I will kill him right now myself. He doesn't want to live? He doesn't get to live," she said and swiped him hard across the face. Stan's head jerked violently to one side

"Will you stop that or I call security."

Aduke broke down on her son and sobbed softly into his face. She held his hand tightly and quietly prayed "Please, please darling. You are the only one I have in this world. Please come back to me. I love you. Even if you don't have Simbi or your job, you have me. You shouldn't have forgotten that. I love you. I love you. Wherever you are now, I need you to know that your mother wants you back."

"It is alright." Doctor Fernandez said. He was deeply touched. He gently lifted Aduke off Stan's unconscious form. "I know this is difficult for you, but you have to make a decision. Of course if you need time...."

"No, Ehm... I have made my decision."

"Okay."

"Do the blood transfusion, doctor. I will take care of him."

"Alright, I will get the papers."

Dr. Fernandez gently led her out of the room.

***

Gossip in the hospital spread like wildfire. From the quiet whisper of nurses who had read case notes to the attendants who picked snippets here and there. In two days, word got to Abigail that Stan

had gone away and was never coming back
She stormed into his room enraged, not caring. Today she wasn't
here to clean or change sheets. She closed the door behind her and
turned the key. She removed the key from the hole and tossed it
away. Now she stood before Stan, looked at him for a long time, until
her anger simmered, until she could breathe again. She bent over him
and delicately kissed his forehead.

"I understand Stan, and I am coming with you," she
whispered.

She retrieved from her pocket a bottle of green liquid
substance, a needle and syringe. She withdrew exactly 10mls of the
substance and injected it into her arm, unflinching.

"I am com-ing- with-you—Stan," she drawled and collapsed
to the floor.

Abigail had gathered gossip on Stan but she did not get to
know about the blood transfusion and the decision Aduke had made
before she travelled.

3

Stan got into his car and took a long deep breath. He felt at peace
with the world. Simbi meant so much to him and he was
tremendously glad that he could now provide for her. Things had
started looking up and it could only get better.

He fired the ignition and his artificial driving assistant came
to life.

"Welcome Stan, how was the office?" A voice came from the
dashboard.

"Hey, Buddy the office can't be better," he fastened his seat
belt.

"I have good news, I better call Simbi," he said and reached
for his cell phone.

"Welcome Stan, how was the office?" Buddy said again.

"You've already said that fool, I will soon have you changed. I have always wanted the new HLG 20 AP."

"Sorry about that."

"Ah, shut up," Stan said.

He dialled Simbi's cell and almost immediately disconnected the call. No, he wasn't going to tell her on the phone. He was going to surprise her, then, they would go out to celebrate. He punched the *MyView* button on his cell again.

The living room was empty except for the dining table that appeared crowded. He zoomed and saw two plates of half-eaten food, two glasses and a bottle of wine, half-emptied. Stan gaped, baffled, there was something about the scenario he did not like. He navigated to the bedroom and was paralysed by what he saw.

Two figures were entangled on the king-sized bed. Stan zoomed in, the number of pixels around the bed rapidly decreased and he could see that Simbi was in bed with a man. Another man. His hand shook violently as he redialled her number. She picked up on the second ring "Yes, darling," she said, breathlessly

"Simbi, who is that in your bed?"

"What?"

"You heard me?"

"Have you been watching me?"

"Simbi, I saw someone in your bed. Who-is- that? Answer me!" Stan screamed.

"Unbelievable. You connected your *MyView* to my bedroom? How dare you invade my privacy. You have absolutely no right."

"And you have a right to sleep with another man when we are getting married in the next two months? Eh, tell me about rights!"

"I am leaving you, that is it."

"No... Simbs. I got a raise, a promotion. Please.'

"I give you twenty four hours to remove your chips from my home, after then, I am calling the police." The line went dead.

"Simbi, wait!"

Stan sat still for a moment. The car engine was still humming; with a rhythm that echoed in his turbulent heart. His hand was covered in sweat as he watched the excitement he had earlier felt evaporate and stream out of his grip. He hit the steering wheel hard with his fist and the car promptly went dead.

"Stan is upset," Buddy said "Calm down or I radio the FRNC. You are unfit to drive."

"Okay, I'm alright now... I'm alright now."

"Heart rate is at 100 beats per minute, you have to go down to 90 maximum." Buddy said.

"What kind of government is this? This is what I have to put up with?"

"The car won't move, till you achieve at least 90 beats per minute, your normal heartbeat is 83 beats per minute," Buddy recited a programmed traffic rule.

Stan took a couple of deep breaths to calm himself down. He felt like smashing the artificial passenger, but he knew he won't get past a hundred kilometres before he would be apprehended. He closed his eyes and pictured an excited Simbi that waiting for him. Yeah, that did the trick.

He heard the engine.

"Where are you going Stan?" Buddy asked.

"Ikorodu, Simbi's apartment."

He manoeuvred the car out of the office block and with every ounce of his being he suppressed the urge to speed off. He carefully drove towards Ikorodu. Suddenly a red light started blinking on the dashboard.

"Your battery is low, your battery is low," Buddy said.

"I can't charge the car now; I will stop at a station when I leave Ikorodu."

"Your battery is low, your battery is low," Buddy repeated.

"Didn't they teach you to just shut up when a man is upset?" Stan said, irritated.

"Your battery is..."

Slam! Stan angrily crushed the delicate device attached to the dashboard. The artificial passenger shattered into bits and pieces. He looked at his hand, hot rage welling up inside of him; he saw the tip of his white shirt sleeve slowly taking on a bright red colour. He knew splitters of glass must have torn his flesh. But he couldn't feel pain now. The only pain he felt was in his heart. He was now beyond himself and ready to damn all consequences. By now he knew the FRNC would have been automatically alerted. The police and the ambulance would trace his car at neck-breaking speed thinking he had been involved in a car accident or worse, attacked. Accident and armed robbery had reduced drastically. More victims had been saved by this prompt response. If he was found to have triggered a false alarm and to have deliberately destroyed the Artificial Passenger, Stan knew he was going to face serious charges, but before then, he had to see Simbi. He had to persuade her to stay with him. Maybe she thought I was lying about the raise.

He estimated ten more minutes before the force caught up with him. He decided to park the car as soon as he got to the next train station. Five more minutes of driving, then he began to hear the distant wail of sirens. He pulled into the parking lot of a mall two blocks away from the station. Switched off the engine and decided to join the underground train to Ikorodu. He ransacked the glove compartment for a train ticket he usually kept handy. He couldn't find it. The siren was nearer. He heaved his suitcase from the back seat and searched for the ticket. He had to find it. He didn't have the time to buy one at the station. Damn! He poured the contents of the case on the floor and documents flew around the car, then he saw what he was looking for. He got out of the car and broke into a run. God! The siren sounded too close.

He was at the station now, and then he saw the police patrol car pull out in from of him. The four doors of the car flew open as the car screeched noisily to a halt. Four uniformed policemen jumped out with their handcuffs, pistols and sticks.
Stan stopped running and raised his two hands. Game over
Suddenly, he felt dizzy, his knees went weak. Then he felt a hand firmly grip his arm.

Have I been shot? That was the last thought on his mind before he faded.
The policemen stopped abruptly. Looked at each other nervously,

not understanding the spectacle of the disappearing man, and ran in different directions.

4

Stan slowly opened his eyes. He couldn't understand why the lids were so heavy. His head pounded and he felt tied to the bed in a hundred places. He didn't bother to move an inch; he knew that wasn't going to be easy. He looked around the room and his heart skipped a beat as he recognised the space.

"What?" he screamed and sat up. Pain shot through all his joints "No, no this is a dream."

"Do not stand up," a voice sternly called out

He jumped in fear and whirled around to see his companion. "Who the hell are you?"

"Lie down."

"The hell I will," he screamed. "Who are you and what am I doing here?"

His companion left the window and sat down in a wicker chair, the only furniture in the room. A fan suspended from the grey ceiling circled tiredly, as if trying to shake off the black dust that clogged its blades, not succeeding, it made a swooshing sound.

"You now live here Stan."

"What?"

The giant clock on the wall had a picture of a man and a woman in their late thirties. They wore *aso-ofi* of the same design, and a happy big grin of the same intensity. The two hands of the clock rose from the hands they joined together in holy union. The hour hand crossed across the belly of the man and the minute hand did the same to the woman, forming two radii in opposite directions. It was a quarter past nine.

Below the picture, was printed in bold lettering:
MR &MRS JACOBS BAMIWO
HAPPY 10th YEAR ANNIVERARY
5th JUNE 1985

119

The wall clock ticked and the hand resting on the bosom of the woman slowly crawled away, making a tick-tock sound as it went.

"Were you married?"

"Are you an idiot? Those are my parents." Stan retorted angrily. "Look, you will have to tell me what is happening, okay. This is my past, a very scary one at that. I don't want to be anywhere here. How did I get here? I am supposed to be in the future not the past."

"I know."

"Then why am I here?"

"I mean your mother. I know her. I met her in the future. Were you married before the accident, before you travelled to 2060?"

Stan was puzzled, "how did you know about that?"

"My name is Abigail. I took care of you when you were hospitalised, after the accident, in 2010 of course. That was when I met your mother. She is broken Stan, why did you do that?"

Stan opened his mouth and nothing came out. The only sound in the room came from the ceiling fan and the wall clock. A rhythm that stuck in his head.

Flap-tick-flap-tock.

He got off the bed and approached Abigail menacingly, "you..." he pointed a finger at her, "you are lying!"

"Why did you do it?" Abigail repeated calmly

"Oh," Stan ran his two hands through his hair and moved away. The floor, where the carpet had torn, felt cold on his bare feet as he went to the window and open the curtain a slit. He regarded the dark empty street for a long time. The street was all too familiar; he could make out every detail the dark sheet of nightfall was trying to hide. He knew the secret of the night. The smell of the dark. The whiff of poverty.

He turned to Abigail "I wanted a different life, a world were dreams can happen. I wanted happiness."

"Happiness? What do you know about happiness? What about the people whose happiness depended on your existence?"

"How did you get here?" Stanley asked.

"Answer me."

"No, you answer me. How did you know I was in 2060, and why did you bring me back to..." Stanley looked around the room and saw the wall clock. "...1985?" Stan was alarmed. "You could at least have taken me back to 2010, this is worse than being caught by the police in 2060. Where did you get the substance by the way?"

"Too many questions for a night." Abigail said and got off the chair.

"Really?" Stan scoffed.

"Look, I think we should get some sleep now. In the morning we have a lot to talk about."

"Sleep? Where? On this single ratty old piece of mattress?" Stanley asked.

"Yes. You slept there for the most part of your life, remember?" Abigail threw back at him and went to lay on one side of the mattress, waiting for Stanley to join her.

Stan felt something invincible but hard hit his gut. "Yeah," he scoffed, "you are right, but don't worry I will take the chair."

"You want to sit the night through?"

"Yes."

"Be my hero."

5

Aduke entered the room with a bowl of tepid water and threw the windows wide open. The morning sun streamed into the room and illuminated two bodies lying on separate beds. She was staunch in her belief that the morning sun contains some vitamins that would do a lot of good to the occupants. Not that the sun would bring them back, but it helped to hope. She began to clean the room

When Abigail was found lying unconscious on the floor after injecting the same substance that sent Stan off on a never-ending journey, everybody was surprised. Everybody but Aduke who knew

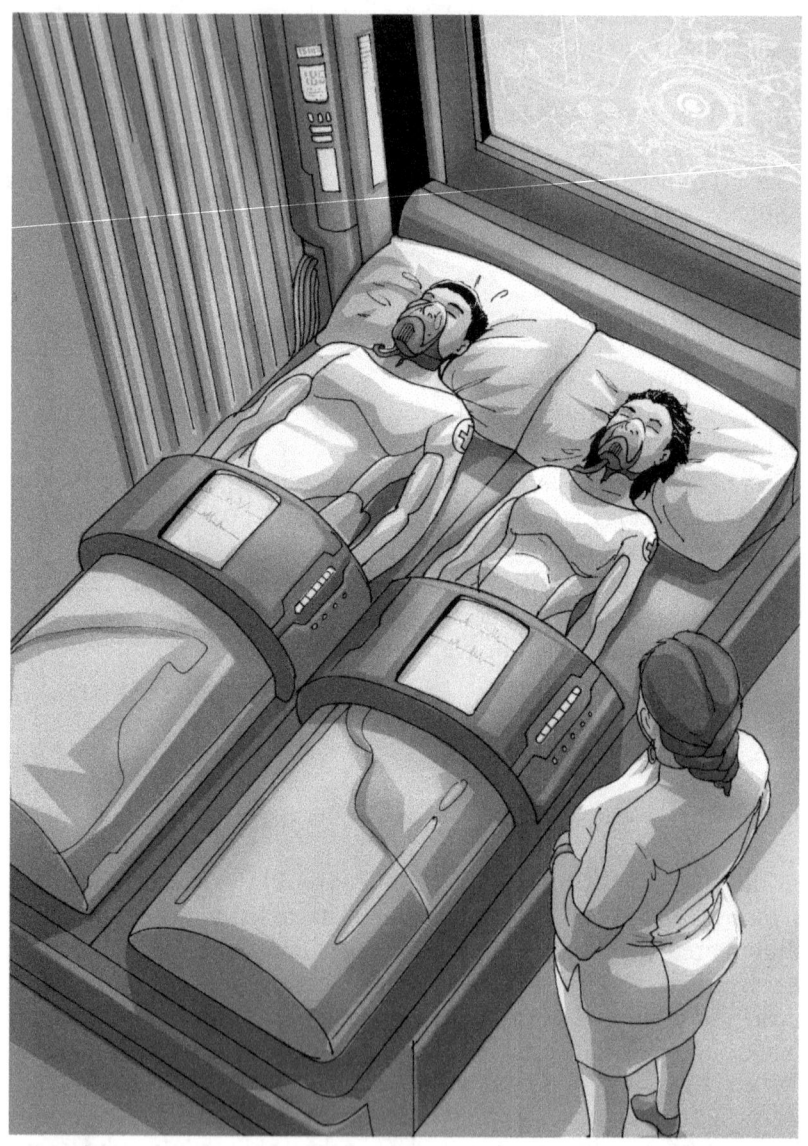

exactly what was happening. She immediately stopped the blood transfusion she had earlier agreed should be performed on Stan. She took Abigail into her home and took care of her when no family member came for her.

Aduke dipped a towel into the bowl of water, squeezed out the excess and began to mop Stan's body. When she was done, she moved on to Abigail and did the same.

By the time she was through, the morning sun was gone. What was left was more of a scorching light that Abigail also staunchly believed should not be allowed to touch the occupants, so she firmly closed all the windows and moved away silently.

She turned at the door and whispered "I am waiting."

It's been a year and a half.

6

The morning was clear and clean because the rain came in the night and washed the dirt away. Farmers rejoiced, creatures crawled out, plants danced and weary souls reflected. Greens were greener, roses were brighter, butterflies were on yellow petals, tiny insects drank from leafy green mugs and Abigail and Stan came out to bath in the clean air.

They walked down a narrow path in the bush, leaving deep footprints in their wake. Though brown mud clogged their feet and occupied the narrow spaces between their toes. They could only feel the cleanliness and purity of it all.

Birds twitted happily over their heads and they could make out the distinct sound of water a short distance ahead.

"So, how come you didn't like it here?" Abigail finally broke the silence.

"Have I said I didn't?" Stan looked at her.

"Not in so many words" Abigail said.

"Why did you bring me here?" Stan asked

"I think you already know."

"To appreciate what I had?"

"You went to 2060 to look for happiness, happiness was here Stan. Can't you see it? Can't you smell it?"

"I never saw it. I never appreciated this life. All I could smell was fish and poverty and then, more fish. My father was a fisherman, my mother a fishmonger. Mother smoked and sold the fish I and my father caught. So you see all I saw and smelt back then was fish in all its forms. But my parents were passionate about education, so they gave me the best they could afford. I went to a boarding school in town, and one day when I came home for a long vacation, I didn't meet my father. He died shortly after I left for school."

The narrow path curved into a bend and Abigail tripped over a shrub "Oh, I am so sorry," he empathised.

Stan helped her up "Are you okay?"

"I'm fine." "Oh," she continued, "that must really have been hard on you and your mother."

"It was difficult. Everything reminded us of him. The water, the fish, even the leaves told his story. So, we left the village. Mother had a primary education, so she got a cleaning job at the Lagos state Civil service Commission. I was the centre of her existence and she worked very hard to see me through the university."

"She must have really loved you," Abigail said.

"Do not judge me lady."

"But what you did was cruel. That was no way to pay her back. She didn't deserve you leaving her like that." she insisted.

"Abigail, I need you to listen to me, not judge." She noticed that he called her name for the first time since they arrived. That was something.

They reached the riverbank and sat down under a palm tree. Fishermen were busy casting nets; women and children were sorting fish, crabs and shrimps into different wicker baskets. A woman chattering excitedly to her peers stopped and glanced at them. She seemed to have said something about them and then continued her chattering.

"It was my father," Abigail said, eyes still fixed on the group of women.

"What?" Stan asked

"You wanted to know how I got the substance. My father discovered it. He was a scientist who had an unwavering belief in herbs, and then one day he stumbled on this leaf. And after a series of lab tests, he declared that the leaf contained a substance that is capable of making time travelling possible."

"Unbelievable! Your father was Dr. Ngozi?""

"Yes, and I cannot believe he gave you the substance. He promised me he wasn't going to give anyone after what happened to me."

The woman stopped chattering and moved towards them.

"You think she knows you?" Abigail asked

"Maybe, what...what happened to you?" Stan looked quizzical.

"Hey my children, I am so sorry to bother you." The woman stood in front of them.

"No problem ma, what can we do for you?" Stan responded, eager to be rid of her.

"Are you from around here? I am not sure I have seen you two before." The woman asked waving a finger at them.

"We are travellers" Abigail said politely.

"Travellers? Where are you going to?

"Ah..." Abigail searched for the appropriate answer.

"You must try my fish soup before you leave anyway. You see, I cook the best fish soup around here. I am renowned for my talent in cooking, some even think I should spend more time cooking than fishing, but I can't do without the water."

"Oh, we would be delighted." Abigail enthused.

"What can we do for you ma?" Stan repeated rather too sharply.

"Thank you, my son. I just received a letter from my son who is overseas, and you see, today is Thursday I will not have time tomorrow to go to the community school so that Teacher Chike can read it for me. And on Saturday, I have a child naming ceremony to

126

attend. Not that it is compulsory for me to go, but the mother of the lady that gave birth is my friend from birth. I mean we are childhood friends. And I could have gone to see teacher Chike at home, but his wife. Ah his wife, you need to know his wife to understand what I am saying. I don't know if the woman thinks as old as I am I can be interested in her husband. Well, not that I still can't go but..."

"Mama, bring the letter." Stan cut her chatter.

"Oh, my son, you know where I was going. You are a good man," she said giggling excitedly. "Ehm let me get the letter," she said wiping her wet hand with the edge of her wrapper, an attempt to remove the fish scales that had clung to her hand. That done, she lowered her wrapper a bit to reveal her hidden pouch. She unzipped the pouch and brought out a parcel tied with rope made from palm leaf. She untied the rope and brought out the letter from a thick nylon envelope. "I have to be careful so that water doesn't touch it. You know we that work in the water, we experience a lot of things. You see that man over there, see, see that one with the face cap, his wife. Hmn, if you know what happened to the wife yesterday. She delivered in the water."

"Ah!" Abigail gasped.

"Yes o. The village doctor had already told her that her time was near, that she should stop coming to the river, but she refused, she is like me. She can't do without the water. Yesterday as we were fishing, all of a sudden, her water just broke. We tried o, before we know what was happening, the boy's head was out, the baby is a boy, so I quickly..."

"Ehm... I am sure it must be really hard. Let me have..." Abigail tried to cut her.

"Ah, my child it is o, but we also enjoy it a lot. As you see me, I don't think I can do any other job. I have been doing..."

"Ok, mama we were about..." Stan started.

"Here, here is the letter. God bless you." She gave Stan the letter and quickly sat down beside him.

Stan read the letter and turned to the woman "Mama, your son says he is doing very fine and he wants you to know that he misses you and loves you so much. But the reason why he wrote the letter was that his wife has delivered a bouncing baby boy. He also..."

"Heh o... my son has a son, I have a grandson!" The woman was overjoyed. She laughed uncontrollably until tears stained her face, then she flung herself on Stan and hugged him tightly. "My son, I am blessed, I am happy, I am so happy." She rejoiced. Abigail observed the drama unfolding beside her and burst out laughing. She joined the woman in rejoicing and they stood up and started dancing.

Stan was glad he was still in one piece when the woman got off him. He made a mental note not to read any more letters around here. That could be a dangerous act. He massaged his neck and started removing fish scales from his clothes where the woman had rubbed him. He patiently waited for the hubbub to subside.

"In fact I have done enough for today, I have to go and tell all my friends," she said, breathless.

"I am sure you have to." Abigail agreed.

"But I am not leaving you here; you must follow me home for the fish soup."

"No, we can't..."

"Of course that would be wonderful, we are famished." Abigail said.

"Abigail!"

"Let's go and have a meal."

"Children, just give me some minutes to get my basket and say goodbye to my friend," the woman said and danced away. Abigail sat beside Stan still giggling. Happiness can be infectious, if you allow your heart to feel.

"You really like it here, don't you?"

She stopped giggling and turned to him "I like it anywhere I find myself."

They watched the woman as she chattered excitedly to her friends. Another round of hubbub erupted as both men and women started dancing and rejoicing.

"That woman is going to take eternity to say 'goodbye' to her friends." Stan sighed.

6

In the last two years that Aduke had brought Stan and Abigail to her home, she had never gone to bed without talking to them. She always had reasons to go back to that room. When Dr. Fernandez told her about her rising blood pressure, they were the first to know. "Stan, Dr. Fernandez wants me to bury your bodies, he thinks you are the major reason for my deteriorating health. Is that true? No, I don't think so. I just have to reduce my stress level," she had said, tears welling up her eyes.

But Aduke's health had deteriorated more than she wanted to concede. She no longer slept well at night, constantly worrying about what might happen to the bodies. She would spring up in the middle of the night believing she had heard something. "Stan, maybe he is awake and cannot find his way in the dark, and - and has collided into something...Oh God, the table in the corridor!" Then she would race to the room, switch on the light, breathing heavily, and the bodies would be there lying side by side exactly as she had left them. She would collapse on the floor and weep her heart out and that would be the end of that night for her.

She now couldn't stay outside the house for a long time, always fearing something bad might happen in her absence. A fire may start. She gave herself excuses, but she didn't know if those excuses were truer than the fact that she could no longer withstand the taunts and sneers of her neighbours. Little children were afraid of her, and older ones whispered to each other and laughed deliriously when she passed by. One day, when she came out of her house, she saw that someone had written in bold lettering with charcoal; GHOST HOUSE - all over her frontage. She spent the entire day cleaning it off.

7

Stan stood by the window and gazed at the starlit sky for a very long time. He couldn't believe what had happened to him in the last two days. He thought he had it all perfectly planned out. What really bothered him was why he had a plan at all. It was so hard for him to believe now that he didn't appreciate the life he had, and that he had thrown everything away in a moment. All I lost was a woman that didn't love me and a job. But I did have a great talent in music, and I never explored it. Maybe I was having frustrations at work so that I could do something else, so I could develop my talent. Be who I was meant to be. God! My mother - poor woman. And to think that I even tried to destroy my body. This is implausible. But the body was saved. Untouched. Why did God give me a second chance? He thought.

Stan recalled how he had raced to Dr. Ngozi's lab after the staff meeting. He had heard that the sales manager was retiring; he knew he was next in line, but he also knew he wasn't going to get it. He knew by instinct.

But when the post was given to his junior colleague, the bitterness he felt was beyond his expectation. His resilience broke down and the potent venom of injustice burnt in his flesh. He heard Simbi's voice and blood began to pound loudly in his ear. "You lack courage Stan, I am sure your Management knows better." She had told him he would never get the post. He desperately wanted to prove her wrong this time. He had relied on his track record, but Simbi was proven right. He was denied. Again.

He felt stripped of his last shred of manliness and hot pain slashed through his heart. He bottled up the pain and let the anger boil in his veins. He needed the power it gave him; he needed to be in this state to do what he had to do. He had to banish all reason to pull through. He had to be courageous.

Stan sighed loudly and turned to Abigail who was sitting on the bed, "Your father was a good man. He didn't give me the substance. I stole a bottle." Abigail looked at him. Her face was expressionless, "Go on."

"I knew he was going to be at the university, so I went to his lab. I knew the combination that opened his safe. I was his favourite student and he trusted me. He loved me, and I betrayed him."

"How did you know about the substance?"

"I was the first person he showed the leaf to, but I laughed it off as one of his fantasies. Five years after I graduated, he invited me to his lab and showed me his complete work; the time travelling substance. It was amazing and he was so enthusiastic about it, I can remember him telling me that 5mls of the substance could transport a person to any universe he holds in mind. He told me he had not yet decided on what to do with it. I congratulated him and never thought about it, until a year later when I returned for it." He moved away from the window and approached Abigail "Do you think he will ever forgive me?"

"No... don't..." Abigail raised a hand and Stan stopped in his track. "...Stay where you are."

"Abigail, I am truly sorry."

"You don't need his forgiveness. He is dead. He spent the rest of his life worrying about what the substance might do to the person that stole it. His work wasn't complete. He was still working on the side effect."

"God... Doctor is dead?"

"He died a year ago."

"What, what do you mean a year, I have only been away for two days."

"Which is two years after tonight." She jumped off the bed and stood in front of Stan "You travelled to another universe in less than three minutes, do you have any idea how fast that was, how fleeting time moves here. A day here is one year in the real world. He died two days after his substance was stolen, which made it a year before I came after you. Now that we've spent another day, by God, he died two years ago."

"We have to get out of here, fast, right now. How do we do that?" Stan asked pacing the room.

"You should have thought of that before you left."

"Abigail, I had no intention of returning."

"And suddenly you have that intention?"

He went to her and held her shoulders "Please, I have to see my mother."

"Okay, maybe you can go. I will stay. I have nobody to go to. You go and meet your mother."

"No, I am not leaving without you."

"I don't think I can make the journey." Abigail's eyes misted over.

"What? Why, Abigail plea..."

"There is something that I did not tell you."

"What?"

She wriggled out of his hold and moved to the window. "I was the first person to use the substance. I was like you Stan, dissatisfied with my life. It had been only me and my father for too long. My mother died when I was five and my father never remarried. He was married to his work. He loved me but he had little time to spend with me. When I was a child, I promised myself that I would marry early and have many children. I swore I would never be all by myself. That dream never happenned Stan. I was thirty-five and still alone. You don't understand what it means to be alone all your life. So when father made his discovery, I decided to escape this lonesome life. I took the substance and travelled to the future. It took my father a year to bring me back. He gave me another injection to neutralise the travel substance. I spent a day in the future and I missed my lonely life like hell. Can you believe that? I was so glad to be back. Father told me I could have done that by myself by just holding the real world in my mind long enough for my brain to interpret the message."

Stan was dumbfounded; he stared at her and urged her to continue, trying to understand where this was leading, why she could not make the return journey.

"When I came back, desires were meaningless to me, I stopped wanting and I stopped searching and I was the happier. I didn't want anything big, I wanted to live a life as lowly as possible to prove to myself I could be happy no matter what, only if I let myself be, and only if I live to give, so I took the job at the hospital."

"You are a brave woman Abigail, and that is why you must return." Stan took her hand and drew her away.

"No, I can't." Her eye brimmed with tears. "You have to go."

"Why... why can't you?"

"Can't you figure?" She wrenched her hands from Stan. "I took 5mls of the substance the first time I travelled. When I came after you, I took another 10mls, I needed my consciousness to be sufficiently dissociated from my body for us to travel together. You travelled with me from 2060 to here. I now have up to 15mls in my blood stream. The substance doesn't wear off, it stays in the blood stream for the return journey. It's like buying a return ticket. That is why we don't need another dose to go back."

"So how does that affect you? Why can't we go right away?"

"Because my blood is now too potent, I may die if I try to return. 5ml is the return ticket, I have 15mls. I am now too removed from my body, if I try to return I may not be able to control it and fade into nothingness. My consciousness may become completely dissipated... I may die. Stan you must go back and destroy my body."

"No, no I can't leave you. There must be a way out. What about the neutralizer your father discovered? I can go back and neutralise you.

"It's the same thing Stan, the neutralizer was built for a 5mls dose, it won't work on me. He was working on the neutralizer for larger doses when he died."

"Oh God, I ..." Stan shook unbelievingly.

"Don't worry about me, I will be alright. I love it here; I love the people, the water and the life. I promise, I will be fine. Besides, what about my body. What if it had been buried? The hospital would have disposed of the body." she made a futile effort to wipe the tears streaming down her face.

"You risked your life for me, now you want me to leave you?" Stan's voice broke, he gently cleaned the tears streaming down

Abigail's face with the back of his hand.

"Stan, I want you to go."

"No, we are not sure you will die if you try to return."

"And we are not sure I won't."

"Abigail, please you've got to try. There may be a chance."

"Stan, I may not have a body to return into. I am sure I don't. It's better for me to stay here and live on, than to try and then die."

"Abigail you are braver than this."

"Stan please go." Abigail buried her head in his chest and wept.

"Abi-"

"Please go. There is nothing more to say." Abigail quickly moved away and forced herself to stop crying.

Stan did not try to close the distance between them. He moved further away to the window. He looked at the sky and saw a lone star and wondered why it had to be alone. Then he turned and faced Abigail "I want you to know that ....I love you and I always will."

"I ..." She could only gasp.

Stan faded away before she could try again.

8

Aduke had fantasised about the return of Stan and Abigail a million times in her mind. She would be in the kitchen and the door to the room will open, she would rushed out and meet Stan and Abigail coming out of the room. Or maybe she would be there to say good night, and then Stan would open his eyes and whisper 'Mama'. They would hug, kiss and cry and Abigail would watch them, fascinated, and then she wouldn't know how to thank Abigail for bringing her son. But what happened was nothing her wildest imagination had prepared her for.

When she entered the room and switched on the light, the first thing she noticed was the crumpled pattern on the sheet where Stan was supposed to be lying. She gaped in disbelief. Blood rushed to her brain and her vision blurred. She had to hold on to something so that she wouldn't fall.

Stan who had opened the window and was gazing at the starlit sky spun around and saw his mother. He crossed the room in one stride and caught her before she reached the ground.

"Mother, Mother!" he desperately called as he carried her to the bed he just vacated.

"Stanley," she said in a very weak voice, not fully recovered from the shock.

"Mama, I am here."

"I waited so long for this day."

"I know, I am so sorry, can you ever forgive me?"

"I forgave you a long time ago," her vision was clearer now.

"How could you? I don't deserve it."

"I did my son, I forgive you."

"Mama, you..."

"Abigail!" Aduke screamed "Stanley, help me up." Stan did as he was told.

"Why Stanley...why is she not awake?" She was distraught.

"Don't worry about her mother, she will be fine."

"What do you mean?"

"Mother, we will arrange for a quiet funeral for her tomorrow. She is never coming back. Thank you for preserving her body. It would have helped if she had known."

"No... no... no!" Aduke began to sob. She went to Abigail and held her hands.

"Mother, she was the best thing that ever happened to me."

"I know, I know. God, I never meant for her to die." Aduke sobbed uncontrollably.

"She is not dead mother, she is just ... never mind, it's so complicated. I will be outside."

Stanley rushed outside the house to where he could see the sky and feel the night air. He looked up to the sky and got lost. There were tiny stars scattered over the sky and huge clouds forming patterns. He watched as the stars drifted towards North and wondered why they were travelling. He followed a particular star and watched as it gradually moved behind a huge cloud. Then it stopped twinkling, it was no longer visible. Stan felt sad for the star that stopped shining.

No, the stars weren't moving, the stars were stagnant. My star must still be there, under the cloud.

He saw that it was the clouds that were drifting. Drifting towards the south, making it seem like the star was moving towards the North. He watched in feverish anticipation as the huge cloud covering his star gradually moved away.

And the star was revealed, shining brighter.

"Oh!" He gasped.

"Stan," he heard someone call at him. The voice was too familiar, as if he was in a dream he never wanted to wake from, he stood still. He didn't want to break the spell.

"Stan."

Silence.

Stan slowly turned and saw the unmistakable figure of Abigail standing by the door. Abigail, this is impossible. Am I hallucinating?

"Abigail," he tried to use his voice.

"Stan, it's me. Yes, I made it." She said and raced to him.

"How? How did...how? I am so happy."

"There was something I had to say to you."

Aduke came out of the house and stood by the door beaming with joy. "I knew she would come back. I believed in her."

"Stan, when you left, it wasn't the same. I missed you so much; I didn't think I could live through another day without you. I knew I couldn't live without you. So I had to try and here I am. It worked. I made it."

"Yes, you did my dear," Stan said and made to seal her lips with his.

"Wait, wait. I came to tell you something."

"There is plenty of time to do that," he finally did seal her lips with his under the starlit sky.

The more obstacles set up to prevent happiness from appearing, the greater the shock when it does appear. One has not only an ability to perceive the world but an ability to alter his perception of it; or, more simply, you can change things by the manner in which you look at them.

S.

COLD FUSION

BY

AYODELE ARIGBABU

THIS WAIT IS KILLING ME. Four hours of combat simulation and four hours twiddling your toes, all strapped in your G suit, surrounded with the smell of Italian leather that suffuses the interiors of the Indira Giovanni remake of a 2015 Phillipe Starke vintage cockpit design. Well, admittedly, not four hours at a stretch. We had the eight hour block of active duty per day, during which we were entitled to a lunch break and we could watch movies, read e-books, write emails or play computer games in the cockpits of our ZX Falcons or anywhere else within the confines of the red zone. Those activities could be interrupted at any time by the siren, that nerve wracking digital racket that was designed in the pits of hell to put you on the edge. At its insistence, you had to hustle in full combat gear into the cockpit if you were not there already, seal the airlock and engage in what would either be a simulated combat sequence or the real thing- war. For the past five days since the code red was put in place, the siren had only summoned us for combat simulation, the cock-pit became a simulator and we engaged in dog fights and short missions designed to keep our reflexes at the desired levels. We were told that the steel dome of the red zone could roll back at any time, opening the sky to us and allowing 300 ZX Falcons to pour out and put in action any of the 56 counter attack flight patterns we had practised to the point of death. Till that happened, we would stay in code red and twiddle our toes in between false alarms and predictable combat simulations. This wait is killing me, I'd rather get on with the fucking war already.

***

Design Pages
12th January, 2060
The Eko Atlantic Airforce base of the State of Lagos has been besieged by dare-devil photo journalists risking life and limb in foolhardy attempts to beat anti intruder systems put in place at the EAA's Red Zone Hangar in an attempt to get images of The ZX Falcon which has captured the imagination of the public since a security leak from the Ministry of Strategic Intelligence and Defence revealed that 1,500 super fighter planes had been secretly developed in a deal between the Eko Defence Industry (EDI) and the Indian manufacturing giant- Zaza Corporation.

***

The Daily Star
14th April 2060
The Nigerian Government continues to consider military action in its long drawn battle with the leadership of the State of Lagos, the former Nigerian capital which has inched closer to declaring a Republic of Lagos over disputes regarding revenue control and the perennial energy crisis.

Spokesperson for the Presidency, Sam Adeeko spoke with journalists at the Aso Villa Media Centre on the outcome of the emergency Federal Executive Council meeting held last Tuesday, "The presidency is not inclined towards negotiating terms for secession with any group or region within the Federal Republic," said Mr. Adeeko. "The founders of this nation fought a bloody war against the splitting of the nation almost a century ago, we will not shy away from our sacred responsibility for upholding the unity of this nation at any cost. Mr. President has only one message for the Governor-General of the State of Lagos, he would do well to desist from this misadventure. Our ultimatum stands, if the artificial borders created since 6th February between the State of Lagos and other neighbouring states are not demilitarised and thrown open to all Nigerians before the 21st of April, Federal Troops will march into Lagos, the current government will be suspended and a state of emergency put in place for as long as is necessary to put some sanity into the place."

Mr. Adeeko left the media centre immediately after making his short speech without fielding questions from journalists. The government of the State of Lagos is yet to react officially to this reaffirmation of the Nigerian government's position. Attempts to get a reaction from Mr. Rafiu Sonibare, the Press Secretary to the government of the State of Lagos via telephone and Satellite Messaging Links (SML) were rebuffed, save for a protracted laugh and a curt phrase- " I laugh in Spanish!"

***

The Daily Star
12th April, 2060
Alhaji Sani Ahmed is never one to bow to pressure. When his Sunny Breweries released their new drink and called it 'Blood of Jesus', they successfully triggered off runaway sales and the first religious crisis in the country in twenty years. Christian fundamentalists attacked Sunny Breweries' plants and depots across the country and destroyed massive stocks of the new energy drink. Alhaji Sani was not cowed. He stood in front of every television camera that cared to make itself available for his tirade and cursed the 'terrorists' to their fourth generations. Asked about the insensitivity towards Christians in naming a soft drink after the Lord Jesus Christ and then going ahead to advertise the product with seductively clad models on billboards and podcasts, the multi-industrialist and CEO of Sunny Breweries asked if the terrorists should not be honoured by having their Lord and Saviour associated with one of his companies. Asked if he would be so flippant if some aspect of his own faith was treated with similar disdain, Alhaji Sani Ahmed retorted in annoyance- "What disdain? What faith? My faith is in Sunny Enterprises International, and by the grace of God, any rodent that

interferes with any of my businesses will be crushed under my heels."

Dear Maero,

I pine for you. I know you will laugh and toss your hair back in that way I love so much. I know you will say, with your nose upturned, that it is your thighs that I miss. Yes, I miss your thighs, the tender cushion they form for my wayward head on stormy nights, but I miss your thighs because I miss you, the you that is in you. I miss the giggle in your voice, the song in your stride, I miss the anger in your eyes when you flare up at my misdeeds, the anger that makes me want to touch your face and knead the tension out of your cheeks.

My sweet Mae, I pine for you. But this job keeps me away, yet it is more than a job, it is a duty to be done. My sweet Mae, we do this to ensure that for every one of us that has a sweet Mae, we can rest our heads in their thighs in future without fear, we can live in peace and comfort with our sweet Maes. I wage war Maero, but only so we can live in peace....

The mail to Maero does not flow, I feel like a priest who having forgotten the right incantations to inveigle himself into his deity's affection, resorts to mumbling mumbo jumbo in the hope that the right set of words would coalesce sometime and do the trick. I can see Maero in my mind's eye, smirking and responding with one-liners: "This sucks," or "You owe me a little more than a badly written mail." I miss my feisty Miss. Loving Maero is like committing to a low intensity war where you always look forward to the next engagement with the enemy but for the wrong reasons.

I'm struggling for a redeeming next line to dictate in my faltering missive when a beep announces the arrival of a freshnote in my message bin. I flick the cursor away from the email I had been dictating, activating the freshnote window with a click. I had permitted myself the fantasy that perhaps Maero had softened enough to write me after what I did to her before I got called away to the Red Zone; however, it was only an invitation from the boys to play Samurai Jets. It was not a bad idea, I looked at the stale mail I'd been dictating which had been flipped to a side of the screen once I activated the freshnote, and I looked at the pulsing graphic that served as background to the Samurai Jets invite. It was not difficult making a choice, Maero would have to wait, maybe after two rounds of Samurai Jets.

I flipped the switch for the booster speakers, the surround sound hissed to life as I punched the let's-play button on the Samurai Jets invite. In a split second, the loud Afro-rock intro to the game filled the cockpit and the small screen on the ZX's windshield exploded in a variety of motion graphics that got your blood pumping at just the right pressure to do some serious airborne damage.

We were permitted electronic mail contact with three key people, family members were the preferred choices for our handlers at the Red Zone however, knowing us for who we were, we were allowed to add one person of romantic interest to the list. I added Maero, my feisty chic. Rumour had it that two of the boys added one another as romantic interests. When the Red Zone suits- we called them suits, those administrative drones- started to query their choices, they backed out and said it was a joke. The bathroom rumour goes that it was not really a joke, they were testing the system to know how open they could be about their thing. Our electronic mail gets 'ironed' out before it gets delivered either way. We know about the 'ironing', we even know the boys -and girls to be truthful- amongst the suits who specialise in the strange art of cleaning our messages of sensitive information that could leak critical intelligence to the wrong hands or keeping our letters from home free of demoralizing or inciting material. We had learnt one of the laws of the Red Zone by heart: the fear of the Iron Suits is the key to eternal life. Apart from sweeping our mails, they file the touchy-feely stuff we churn out and have their Psy-Suits sift through them for evidence of mental imbalance, and propensity to defect or screw up the Red Zone's operations in any other way. Yeah, whatever, fuck'em!

Cold Fusion. I remember eleven years ago when the science community got all the newspapers excited about the new technology. I was in my first year in secondary school and despite all the hue and cry, it seemed a pretty simple bit of technology to me, scientists in Lagos had, in collaboration with Indian scientists devised an ingeniously cheap means of generating electricity from sea water. It was like the car battery that had been in use for over a century, only replace the acid with sea water and voila- an incredible source of electrical energy presents itself. So they rejigged the car battery with an improved version of a technology the Americans had been making noise about for a long time with no results to show, and made even more noise over it. Big deal! It was much later that I began to understand the implications of the cold fusion batteries.

The government of the State of Lagos bought up the technology and soon enough, the considerable burden placed on the national power grid by Lagos was reduced by half as private individuals acquired cold fusion batteries that afforded them uninterrupted power supply for eighteen months at a stretch. Soon, industrial-sized cold fusion batteries were introduced by the Lagos Metropolitan Government run Eko Energy Corporation (EEC) for the manufacturing industries that had started mushrooming in Lagos since massive tax breaks and other incentives were offered to fledgling manufacturing companies. Within a year, the EEC was generating more revenue for the Lagos Metropolitan Government than any other revenue source. Though cold fusion produced virtually inexpensive energy, the patents surrounding its development were so tightly structured that the batteries could only be sourced from the EEC and each battery was registered in such a way that allowed the government to earn energy tax from the owner. Though the tax was very affordable compared to the bills being charged by the Nigerian Power Commission, despite its inefficient electricity grid, within a year, such a large percentage of the citizens of Lagos had switched to the 'cold batteries' as they were commonly called, that the government witnessed a spike in its internally generated revenue and it became clear, that whatever projections they had made were far below the real potential of the thing.

The problem started when the Nigerian government tried to get a piece of the pie, waving the 1979 Energy Act where energy production and the regulation thereof was vested in the federal government. A massive court case ensued with the armada of lawyers representing the Lagos Metropolitan Government arguing that the EEC was registered legally to produce batteries and if the batteries provided competed effectively against the Federal Power Grid, it was a pleasant coincidence which Lagos and its citizens were determined to benefit from. No law had been contravened; other companies had produced batteries in Nigeria for over a century without government interference in their business. The EEC's batteries might have much higher capacities (the Federal Government's lead counsel, a grizzled 70-year-old veteran snorted loudly at the sarcasm) than any other batteries ever manufactured in Nigeria...anywhere in the world for that matter, but batteries they were and the EEC, though state-owned, still had every right to have the manufacturing and sale of its products protected by the law of the land, especially given the widespread application and benefits the product was already delivering to the populace. The Feds wanted the EEC to divest itself of its grip on the cold fusion patent, handing over its rights to the Federal Power Energy Commission as a central regulatory body so the batteries could be sold across the country and its benefits made available to every Nigerian. The EEC argued that though they had plans to sell the batteries beyond Lagos, however they were not prepared to let go of their patent. The legal battle continued for eighteen months and got overtaken by political battles, with claims of attempts at industrial espionage from Lagos and claims of economic sabotage from Nigeria. Soon enough, the Governor-General of the State of Lagos, in a move announced to be an attempt to reduce cases of multiple taxation being borne by Lagos citizens announced that every citizen's tax file would be loaded on an identity chip. The Lagos Identity Chip- LIC would also carry other information such as driver's license, credit information, health information and more, to make it easier to manage the tax information alongside all other personal data. Within six months of the introduction of this streamlined database on identity chips, it became impossible to visit Lagos and enjoy any advantages the city-state had to offer without acquiring a Lagos Identity Chip. You couldn't own a house; enjoy cheap public transportation; and more importantly, own a cold battery, without a LIC card. Soon enough, many Nigerians acquired LIC cards and became Lagos citizens, albeit virtual citizens, all for the chance to buy a cold battery. There were reports of some black market trade, but this was hard to sustain as each battery was wired to a central data centre that was monitored by the EEC. If your battery was stolen, it could be remotely deactivated once you sent in a report.

In July 2059, the Federal Government got impatient and engineered the passage of a law that sidestepped all the technicalities contained in the constitutional amendments made in 2032 and the Energy Act of 1979, which had made it impossible for their lawyers to stop the sale of EEC's batteries, by essentially legislating that the EEC could no longer exist except as an arm of the Federal Energy Commission. Before the Lagos Governor-General could react to this, the EEC office complex was stormed by a combined team of Secret Service and Special Police and would have been taken over on that same day, save for a pre-emptive move that had been put in place five years before, and not even the Federal Government would have thought Lagos would have ever dared to attempt. For five years, under the guise of a state security programme to combat urban crime and occasional threats of terrorism, the State of Lagos had embarked on special training for a detachment of five hundred security operatives who were thought to be a special police unit. What the outside world did not know was that this was a preliminary move in the making of what would later become known as the Red Zone. This was the beginning of the city's elite army. When the Federal Secret

Service and Special Police agents stormed the EEC's Eko Atlantic City Complex, they were repelled with what was documented to be unprecedented force. Three special agents died in that encounter, yet beyond slight references in the press referring to a misunderstanding between security forces at the EEC Complex, there was no media coverage of what ordinarily should have been sensational news. The Secret Service was embarrassed and puzzled by how they had been so easily overpowered to say the least. The Federal Government read the resistance to their security detail as an act of aggression and gave the EEC an ultimatum to hand over control of its facilities to the Federal Energy Commission. Two more attempts to take over the facility were met with more bloodshed and it became apparent that Lagos had dug in for a bitter fight. The EEC's administrative offices were moved off the Eko Atlantic City to the facility off the coast of the Atlantic where rumours had been rife that some high powered installation had been under construction for the past seven years. It took a while before some information leaked as to the nature of what was now being publicly called the Red Zone, a near mythical security base built off the coast of the Atlantic to protect the city from aerial and amphibious attacks. What the public did not immediately know was that the EEC's Cold Fusion laboratory and factory was located right underneath the Red Zone. The city was committed to defending its energy investment by all means.

Hostilities reached a peak when a naval unit was deployed to try to take over the Red Zone. Both sides managed to maintain a media blackout over the incident, but the story behind the lack of a story was that the Nigerian Navy met with a huge loss without a shot being fired by either side- a major loss of face. The S.S. Bayero which had been a reliable vessel to the Nigerian peace keeping mission during the 2056 uprising in Cape Town was boarded even as Vice Admiral Shafau Emecheta who commanded the mission was attempting to negotiate a peaceful handover of the Red Zone with its handlers, believing he held the position of strength with such a warship in his command. While the voice from the microphones on his command deck which spoke on behalf of the Red Zone asked him to offer one justifiable reason why his invasion of the Red Zone on behalf of the Federal Government should not be viewed as a criminal act, he looked up from his command console to stare into the nuzzle of an RX12 smart riffle held by an operative clad in black oilskin, still dripping water and wearing a mask. His command deck was soon crowded with five more such operatives. Shafau was escorted to land enroute the state prison in Ikoyi with his crew disarmed but unhurt except for a lieutenant with misplaced bravery who had tried to jump one of the operatives and was rewarded with five fractures in two limbs for his effort. "I swear, I didn't see him move, I didn't even know he'd done anything to me till I felt the pain when I still tried to move," he would tell his ward mate at the military hospital on Awolowo Road weeks later, when recounting his encounter with the Red Zone's finest, while recuperating under close surveillance.

Another ultimatum would follow this blatant resistance to federal might, Lagos would respond to this by announcing an edict on the 6th of February 2060 that every non-resident wishing to enter Lagos without an LIC card would have to apply for an electronic pass. To signify his seriousness, the Governor-General commissioned fifty checkpoints equipped with electronic scanners, automated barriers and heavily armed personnel to enforce the edict at all the entry points into Lagos. The Federal Government found it unacceptable and gave a new ultimatum for the dismantling of the borders, failing which the continued existence of the borders would be interpreted as an act of war and would be treated as such.

That in a nutshell is what has led us to this shit that has left me twiddling my toes, playing computer games and writing misguided love letters in what is probably the best kept secret of a military installation on the planet, .

***

The Daily Star

25th April, 2060

The crisis that has rocked Northern Nigeria for the past weeks has reached a new peak with open clashes now being constantly reported between security operatives and armed Christian fundamentalists. The Christians are seeking to destabilize Alhaji Sani Ahmed's different business concerns. His company- Sunny Breweries precipitated the crisis in January with the release of their controversially named energy drink called – Blood of Jesus. The fundamentalists are calling for a stop to the production of Blood of Jesus and are also asking for an unreserved apology from Alhaji Sani to the Christian faithfuls for dishonouring their faith. Alhaji Sani has however vowed to defend his business concerns through every means necessary. He has currently engaged Isreali private security guards at all Sunny Enterprises International installations in the country together with special patrol teams of military and police personnel.

In related news, our reliable sources confirm that the State Security Service has been drafted by the Federal Government to look into the operations of the Christian fundamentalist group with a special mandate to dismantle the group's command structure in the shortest possible time, and quell the unrest that the group's unprecedented activities against Sunny Breweries have created in several major cities in Nigeria. This line of action from the government is said to have been taken after several meetings with Alhaji Sani failed to yield fruit as the business mogul reportedly threatened to arm his staff and take the battle to the fundamentalists if the federal government continued to pressurize him to stop his legitimate business, rather than ensuring the security of law abiding citizens and tax paying business concerns.

Meanwhile, with the current preoccupation with the Sunny Breweries conflict, the deadline set by the Federal Government for the Governor-General of Lagos to dismantle all borders between the State of Lagos and the rest of the country has passed unnoticed. Our sources confirm that the Federal Government would be announcing a new deadline as its security operatives bring the Sunny Breweries conflict under control and free the nation's resources for addressing other pressing security matters.

***

It is tempting to say that the Nintendo Wii was a precursor to kinetic games like Samurai Jets, but that is as glib as saying sticks and stones were the precursors to guided missiles and electron bombs. The tennis playing and go-kart racing functionalities that the Wii brought to the early 2000s is a far cry from the mayhem that Samurai Jets brings to gaming, One doesn't need a degree in game history to see how the Wii's adoption of available motion capture technologies at the time and the direct metaphor that the Wii remote and hand strap, collectively called the Wii nunchuks, derived from the Nunchaku - the Okinawan weapon of choice that gained popularity via the ancient Bruce Lee films - all seemed to have dovetailed into the airborne fighter game that was now the rave in the Red Zone.

Samurai Jets works with advanced motion sensing systems developed by Adrenaline- the Canadian gaming system specialists - composed of virtual gloves, and scalable to include virtual 3D goggles, vest and ankle straps, all made of nothing more than 3D generated laser nodes and vertices that adjust to fit the gamer's physique and which any gamer worth his points would be familiar with. Interestingly, the game synched quite well with our own standard issue G-suit's inbuilt motion sensor functionalities, albeit that our G-suits were built on more advanced technology, which is why the game spread so easily through, the Red Zone. It felt like it was created for us, in fact that was what we thought, that the Suits had found a way to get us to put in more practice time. We were not complaining, we were having fun.

It's not called Samurai Jets for nothing. You actually do fight like a Samurai, but with jets. You could make your plane do almost anything your body could do, naturally, the more acrobatic you were, the more exploits you could achieve with your jet in the air. You squeezed a virtual trigger on the virtual joystick in your palm to release an energy pulse that chased after your opponent's jet like a guided missile. Backflips and cartwheels were allowed as long as you could maintain your sense of direction in 3D space. To fly in a certain direction, all you had to do was to point the virtual joysticks in both palms in that direction and squeeze. It was as easy as that. "In Samurai Jets, you are presented with the all-time best of gaming entertainment in an extremely immersive environment as the 1986 movie *Top Gun* meets with the 1993 computer game- Mortal Combat; with topnotch 2060 digital technologies from Adrenaline." That was how one of the game trailers put it and that was exactly how it felt playing the game.

I'd thought I would put in two rounds of Samurai Jets before calling it quits, but I was now on my fifth round. In a manner akin to our flight cadet training days, before we earned our wings at the Red Zone, the game was so immersive you lost track of time like we did in the flight simulators just enjoying the novelty of simulated flight before the introduction of serious combat into our flight routines replaced all the romantic notions with the grimness of an adrenaline fuelled determination to stay alive. Our flight simulators just like the ZX Falcons they mimicked were built on Indian technologies, from hardware to software. There was internal gossip that Adrenaline, the Canadian Motion Capture specialists had threatened to sue the Zaza Corporation alongside the Eko Defence Industry for unauthorized use of some of their key source codes in the development of the ZX flight control systems shortly after the security leak that put news of the ZX Falcon in the press. Subsequent gossip however suggested that the disagreement was settled behind closed doors and we never heard anything about it ever again. We naturally assumed, when Samurai Jets invites started to pop up on our consoles, that the inclusion of the game on our down-time entertainment menu was a subtle part of that settlement-behind-closed-doors. How wrong we were! We thought we were only doing beta testing for a new game manufactured by a company associated with our employers, even if by behind-closed-

door-settlements, in that regard, we were right, at least in a certain sense.

Samurai Jets brought back memories of our flight cadet training days in another sense. My background came to bear during training and particularly when everything came together in simulated combat, I had such an aptitude for the razor sharp reflexes and stamina required to stay on top of dogfights that I soon earned the position of Alpha Dog in my squadron, a position I still maintain. To be Alpha Dog, you have to be the overall best at dog fights and have the ability to lead your squadron to success against enemy squadrons. I credit the former to the rigorous martial arts training I imbibed during my childhood which accelerated the advanced mixed martial arts training we received as cadets. The latter I credit to my genes, I picked up strong leadership skills from my father who dominated every industry he ventured into. I grew up with an iron will. I was fast becoming the Alpha Dog at Samurai Jets as well. We all signed in with pseudonyms and randomly arranged ourselves into teams for the tournament mode.

I had once again taken down more rival jets for my team and was considering continuing into a sixth round when a sudden *freshnote* interrupted my play. Red Zone business always superseded any personal activity, even an exciting play of Samurai Jets. The *freshnote* announced that the shore leave I applied for had been granted and I had a pass to leave the Red Zone for 24 hours for family business. Transport had been arranged to take me to the city and I had fifteen minutes to take it. It was an order. At the Red Zone, almost everything you were told was an order. The only problem was that I had not applied for any shore leave for family business and I knew of only one person that fit the description of 'family' who would make it his business to arrange shore leave for me without my asking for it. He might have paid for my martial arts training and a good deal of my education, but I was getting tired of his meddlesomeness. I signed out on my console and kicked out of the harness. It was time to hit the city and straighten out some issues once and for all.

***

Years ago, I once stumbled on an e-book, an old play by the legendary playwright N'duro D'asiko where he bellyached about the tardiness of Olokun - the goddess of the ocean - who wallowed in self-importance and harassed its subjects for endless sacrifices to assuage one petty transgression or the other while under its very nose, ships from distant shores rode over its primary domain- the Atlantic and wreaked untold havoc on its subjects by carting their brightest and strongest away as slaves. The playwright wondered how irresponsible a god could be in abandoning the subjects it was duty bound to protect at the most critical moment in their history and still have the guts to expect continued loyalty. If Olokun had been the head of a corporation, drawing fat salaries, allowances and benefits, she would have been disgraced and summarily fired or even tried for negligence, so ran the central thread of N'duro D'asiko's play. I replayed that thread in my mind as I made the crossing from the Red Zone to the Southern Shore Jetty of the Eko Atlantic City aboard a Yokohama Sting Ray, the speed boat of choice for ferrying personnel on or off the Red Zone. I was the first of the Japanese vessel's five passengers to leap unaided off the boat as it berthed. Niceties were not necessary on those short shuttles as everyone carryied their secrets close to their hearts. I wasn't interested in them or their secrets. I had issues of my own to resolve and I didn't have a lot of time.

Street trading was banned in the Eko Atlantic City, but at transport nodes like the Southern Shore Jetty, itinerant traders still appeared at your elbow offering you an array of products from shoe polish to sanitary pads. I made a line through them, worked my way through security control at the habour gates after passing my Red Zone security pass through their sensors and found an unmanned taxi rank just outside the gates. I was careful to avoid the DADA vehicles which littered the rank like a plague and opted for a two wheeler instead. I chose a Japanese brand, a retro-fitted Suzuki and swiped my LIC card through the terminal to release the break locks. The bike came to life immediately I kicked it, its sensors having locked onto my LIC card after swiping and initiating a metre upon which I would be charged for my usage of the bike.

It was good to be in the city again, the city of my birth, I rode through its streets, weaving the bike past towering office complexes and condominiums that housed the rich and powerful. I noticed that the strong air of pride that permeated the city still held sway. Everyone felt proud in Eko Atlantic City, the rich and powerful businessmen and politicians and the not-so-rich-and-powerful everyday people who kept their businesses and their politics in shape. Everyone felt proud, even the buildings were designed with pride in mind. Decades ago, a bunch of businessmen and politicians decided to build a city every African would be proud of, they chose to build it on the ocean under the pretence of reclaiming land that had been eaten away by ocean surge, but the real reason for pushing the frontiers of the engineering and architectural skills of the era was pride. A similar thing had happened in Dubai just before the Eko Atlantic City dream. The Lagos politicians and businessmen had visited Dubai several times, they had seen the man-made islands in the languid sea, nay, they had bought houses on some of those islands, they were fed up of only being able to find what their money could afford them in foreign countries. They were tired of the patronizing way the Emiratis would sidle up to you when they knew you had a stack of money to burn on their real estate deals, while insulting your Nigerian heritage behind your back during their tea break gossip. Their pride got the better of them and they decided to build a city of the future in their backyard. They raped the ocean and it obliged them by giving birth to a dream city.

I rounded a bend at the city-centre and stopped momentarily to behold the building that was my destination. Dream Towers: a pair of massive stainless steel tubes stuck into the ground at diametrical angles- one tilting towards the east and the other, the west- and connected with a massive red LED mesh that constantly played back an array of digital content. Sometimes horrifying to look at, sometimes awe inspiring, sometimes garish, sometimes beautiful, always overwhelming. I wondered for the umpteenth time what he was trying to say, not the architect who designed the building, but the man who commissioned the architect, the man who had the guts to demand that such a building be conceived, and then built. I had never asked him and I was not going to ask him that question today. I rode into the building's underground parking bay to park the bike and took a long flight of steps to the reception hallway. The afternoon was far spent and I was the only one trying to go up in the hallway. The elevators opened intermittently to disgorge different smartly dressed staff leaving the building after the day's work while I did battle with the digital receptionist that would either agree to give me an e-pass to ride any of the elevators to see whoever it was I desired to see or turn me back with a polite request to make an appointment.

Do you have an appointment? It asked. I gambled and clicked yes. The computer's avatar on the keypad seemed to roll it's eyes as the computer searched it's data banks for a match between the details on my LIC card and any appointment that might have been made in that name. Finally, it obliged me with a curt: "Welcome to Dream Towers Mr. Kamorudeen. You may now advance to the 56th floor through an elevator of your choice. Kindly desist from exiting at any other floor as this may trigger off our intruder alert system. Have a good day." Yeah, fuck you, I thought as I picked an elevator from the pool to ride up in. The cocky old geezer, I thought to myself, he actually booked an appointment for me, he actually took it for granted that I would come without him directly asking. The elevator opened up at the 56th floor even before my mind had finished framing the thought. I stood in the elevator lobby for a bit gathering myself together. The walls were white and spotless as usual and the nauseating smell of organic paint hung in the air. He said it was better than petrochemical paints because it was not carcinogenic. I thought it smelt like shit, no matter how much he said it cost.

"Welcome Mr. Kamorudeen, it has been a long time since the last time you paid us a visit here, the boss has been expecting you." The digital sound came through concealed speakers, but I had been expecting it and was a little surprised that it took its time in acknowledging my presence. "How are you Peter, I see you've just had a paint job done." "Yes," the electronic voice replied, "it was time for our scheduled touch up just two days ago." "Is he alone?" I asked, something told me he wasn't and Peter confirmed it. "No the boss is not alone, Alhaji Sanni is with him, but he left instructions that you were to come in immediately you arrived." Alhaji Sanni? He wouldn't be there if what the old man wanted to see me about had nothing to do with him. I didn't bother trying to conjecture what the two old geezers had up their sleeves; I headed for the chrome handles on the only double door that opened out of that lobby. "Thank you Peter, I'll go in now." "Very well sir." I only faintly heard the slightest whirr as Peter unlocked the anti-ballistic doors just seconds before my hand turned touched the door handle.

***

The cavernous room took most of the 56th floor of the west tower and felt even more spacious than it actually was, what with the sweeping glass wall that enveloped it, leaving an uninterrupted view of the Eko Atlantic City as a conspicuous backdrop. At times, the Atlantic could be sighted in between the buildings, giving the whole array a surreal feel. I spotted Alhaji Sanni standing by the glass wall staring past two adjoining towers, past the Atlantic, into nothingness. He wore his customary robe; the babanriga which few people like him still wore outside of ceremonial events. He wore it well though, always folding the sleeves with deft flicks of his hands and moving so smartly in it like a Samurai in a Kimono. "Good evening Alhaji," I murmured. He looked in my direction and nodded in acknowledgement, intoning "How are you Dami?" in his deep drawl before resuming his contemplation of nothingness.

I left Alhaji to his meditations and swivelled my eyes to where I knew I'd find 'him,' right there in the centre, where all the kinetic whorls and lines that patterned the floor converged in a circle of white space. In the middle of that white circle was a black silk rug on which he was perched with one leg folded under him and the other stretched out while he gave the ipad 12 on his lap all his attention, as if he was not aware that I had entered. "Hello Father." I offered, wondering how he kept it up all these years, sitting alone on his black mat in the middle of this white space surrounded with nothing but glass, and the city skyline. He never had any furniture in the place unless he was meeting with a few important people he considered worthy enough to admit into his 'think room', as he likes to call it. On other occasions, he would offer you a mat on the floor, if you declined, he wouldn't take offence, but you'd have to stand while you conversed with him. "Just a minute," he grunted without looking up, jabbing into the device on his lap to send or request some information. Once when I still felt beholden to him, I had attempted to replace the antique gadget, the last model that Apple Corporation would release before discontinuing the line in 2032, with a more nifty and modern Qyuintax memory slate; he had resisted the move with such vehemence I had felt offended, I never tried to upgrade his personal infotel equipment ever again. Done fiddling with the ancient gadget, he looked up at me and smiled with his simmering silver hair forming a halo around his head and his stringy beard giving his jaw a distended look.

"Hello Oluwadamidada, thank you for coming, I trust you are well?" I deigned not to answer and stared instead at Alhaji Sanni wondering what had brought the effervescent business tycoon to meet with the old man this evening and why my presence was so important to the meeting that the old man would pull the strings he had at the Red Zone to get me out at such short notice. Seeming to have an inkling as to my thoughts, Alhaji Sanni sighed and turned his gaze towards me.

"He is well Sir Alex, look at him; he is well taken care of by the state, perhaps a bit too well that he's started to ignore his father. Dami, the man just asked you if you are well."
"I heard him Alhaji, I didn't realize it was a question, of course I am well."
"Ah, Allah be praised. We need you to be in very good shape Dami, your father and I have a grave task to entrust in your hands, I know your mind is spinning in circles trying to understand why we sent for you. Now Sir Alex, perhaps we should get straight to the point....there is barely enough time as it is."

The old man chuckled on his perch and raised a hand in protest.

"Ah, Alhaji, this is where we always differ, there is always enough time. We shall get straight to the point, but not before I've had a chance to entertain my son whom I have not seen in a long while and in whom I am well pleased. Would you like a drink Dami?....Hush Alhaji...I called this meeting, we shall be civil about its proceedings. Dami, I shall get you a drink..."

He rose from his perch with surprising agility, gathering the tails of his flowing kaftan in one hand. After all the years I've known him, his ability to switch from complete repose to a physically excitable state still never fails to amaze me. He chose to ignore me mumbling about not wanting a drink and went to a section of the wall to punch a code on a keypad no one else would notice in the wall panelling. A portion of the panelling slid aside to reveal a compact bar from which he proceeded to mix me a drink.
"We are cultured people. A guest should not be left with a parched throat. I shall mix you a vintage cocktail of my making, the secret of which I would have sold to Sonny Breweries save that they

159

hypocritically insist on not selling alcoholic beverages. So sad, I would have made Alhaji Sanni here much richer than he is already. You will like this I assure you...did I ever tell you I studied to be a mixologist at the Grande Hotel 'De Italia in '36? That was just before you were born. You know, I was inspired by the Chapman, the creator was never acknowledged and the story is all but forgotten, but we gave the Chapman to the world. Samuel Alamutu, the first Nigerian to run a hotel chain in Nigeria in the 1970s invented the drink. I have spent a lifetime studying the Chapman and now I've put a twist to it. Here....take your time with it, roll it over your tongue...."

I took the cocktail glass from him and sipped from it, watching his animated eyes over the rim with a certain sense of dread. The apprehension proved unnecessary, it was a neat drink that got better with each sip.

"You like it ehn? I knew you would. I call it the Cold Fusion, I've got it patented and I'm going to have it bottled in Alamutu's honour. I'm afraid Sonny Breweries will have to face some competition, they had the first rights of refusal so they should be able to live with it."

Alhaji Sanni cleared his throat and left his spot by the glass wall to approach us.

"Sir Alex, I do not want to sound impatient, but the matter at hand is critical. Perhaps I should brief Dami on why we are here?"

"But that's what I was about to do...."
"We don't have that much time Sir Alex."
"Fine Alhaji, go ahead and tell him yourself."

With that he gathered his kaftan around his knees and lowered himself to his black mat, occupying himself again with the iPad while Alhaji Sanni led me by the arm to his preferred spot by the window while he spoke to me in a low and urgent tone.

"You are old enough to know how your father built his wealth, from a small concern manufacturing toys and corporate gifts in the 30s, he's steadily built the DADA corporation into what it is today. His move into heavy industry was precipitated by a chance meeting with the Indian scientist- Ravi Shukhavati in New Delhi in the summer of 2046. You know the story, Shukhavati's brilliance found an accomplice in your father's madness. They met at a bar in Connaught Place and talked till late in the night. The next morning, your father cancelled the order he had made for 3,000 data chips for a range of customized kiddie phones he was developing for the Christmas season back home. He bought Ravi a plane ticket to Lagos instead and two years down the line after repeated trips between New Delhi and Lagos, the first DADA Road Dragon was granted a license by the Nigerian Automotive Commission."

"You know the story, so why am I repeating it to you? Because Ravi's work is central to what we're here to discuss. You see, what made the Road Dragon such a hit, apart from its iconic design was its legendary fuel efficiency. What nobody knows out there is that the Road Dragon carried a very early version of what is now called the cold battery alongside its fuel cell, thus it was a hybrid vehicle. What I am telling you is that the DADA Road Dragon was an excuse created by your father to test- run the Cold Fusion technologies that Ravi was developing. The tests proved successful and here we are today. What nobody also knows is that early in 2048, your father was able to convince the State of Lagos to provide counterpart funding for further development of the Cold Fusion system under a secret pact...Aha, you start to see where I'm headed? Everything, the Redzone, the ZX Falcons, everything has your father's imprint on it. It was dangerous work, once word got out that Cold Fusion had become a reality on Nigerian soil, a web of global intrigues was triggered off. The Americans wanted in; the Iranians wanted in; the Chinese wanted in. Everybody wanted the technology. There were three kidnap attempts and one assassination attempt on Ravi's life. He has since gone into hiding. Your father was wise; he knew the DADA Corporation, no matter how big it grew, could never sufficiently protect such an important technology. He got the buy-in of the state to protect Cold Fusion from being snatched up by foreign interests and then made too expensive for the African continent. He had tried to get Federal backing, but you know how it is with our people, if it sounds too highfalutin, they would simply shoot it down. Luckily for him, the Governor-General of the State of Lagos then was an astute businessman and an experienced politician. He has made this city what it is today. Unfortunately, the new man in charge is in a hurry, which is not that much of a bad thing, but his pride gets in the way. This crisis with the Federal Government need not have happened."

"Dami, we have called you here because there is going to be a war, and we need you to stop it."
The old man had spoken from his perch without looking up from his iPad. I spun round to look at him, surprised that he had followed what Alhaji Sanni was saying despite the low tone. His face bore a totally different countenance now, he looked deathly serious. He rose quickly in that startling manner of his, came over to where we were and placed a hand on my shoulder.

"We received incontrovertible intelligence that the Federal Government would strike tonight. We had no time, we have no time. If we had more time, I wouldn't have summoned you, but as it is, we need someone inside to turn this thing around the way we want it. The Governor-General has ceased taking my advice; he thinks I've grown old, that I don't understand the way the world works today. I shall have to force his hand. We cannot afford to have a war. The Americans are waiting on the wings to pick the pieces after we're done bombing ourselves. Their aid and rescue missions to save the warring African savages will aid and rescue their own economy by getting to the bottom of our Cold Fusion technologies. It's the same with the Chinese and the Iranians. The Indians are our friends, but they cannot risk too much. We have enough technology to hold off the Feds, but the damage will be almost irreparable. We must not have this war Dami, the Red Zone must not be breached. It remains a strong possibility despite everything the Red Zone has in place; the Feds are determined to get in. We can give you the key to stop this from happening."

"This is what we need you to do..."

Alhaji Sanni took over from the old man in his characteristic alternation between the deep intonation and the urgent low tone. By the time he was done, I was even more agitated than when the old man had offered me a mysterious cocktail he claimed to have invented himself.

"Alhaji, you know I am a military agent and this implies treason?"
"You already committed treason against the Federal Government when you signed up with the Red Zone. The real treason is seeing an opportunity to stop death and destruction and to walk away from that opportunity in deference to fear."
"Alhaji is this really about death and destruction or about the protection of business interests?"

Perhaps I shouldn't have allowed that to slip through, at least not at Alhaji, but it was all coming at me pretty fast and I had to clarify all impressions. Alhaji recoiled like he'd been struck and rolled his eyes in their sockets, replying me in words that sounded like he was spitting expletives despite the fact that they were rendered with civility.

"It is in our business interests to prevent death and destruction!"

I tried another tack...

"Alhaji...this is serious..."

The old man exploded in an unexpected burst of mirth, startling even Alhaji Sanni who otherwise hardly gets startled by anything.

"Ha-ha-ha....This is serious? My son, you are a fighter jet pilot, you're trained in five deadly martial arts, you're a soldier, yet you want to shame me and be a wimp when destiny beckons? This is serious? Do you know what Alhaji has single-handedly done in the service of this our third movement? He has put a business he built for forty years on the line. We orchestrated the 'Blood of Jesus' crisis as a decoy, to distract everyone so we could have more time to perfect our plans...do not let me go into the personal risks and actions I've undertaken in furtherance of this enterprise. Of course this is serious! Do we look like a bunch of unserious old men to you?"

Something struck me in what he had just said.

"You had a hand in the Blood of Jesus crisis?"
"Literally..."

I was looking at him in disbelief, but for once he was avoiding my eyes.

"Don't tell me you..."

Alhaji Sanni confirmed my fears.

"Yes, he came up with the recipe for the energy drink, the name, the whole idea, I backed it all up with Sonny Breweries resources, it worked brilliantly, we even managed to turn a profit despite all the chaos, your father is a genius."

The old man jumped at this with excitement.

"You know I'm a genius, so why don't you want to buy my recipe for Cold Fusion? The drink will be a hit, it has historical precedence, even the name has contemporary precedence...I'm too old to start this sort of business from scratch, you're already in the industry, just stop being sanctimonious for once and let's do good business together..."

"Sir Alex, Sonny Breweries deals in only non-alcoholic brews, it's our unique selling point and we are not ready to dilute the brand with a confusing line extension just to accommodate your wild Cold Fusion project. By the way, the last thing you introduced into the market named Cold Fusion has left us in a mess we're still struggling to get out of."

"Now you know that is not fair, Cold Fusion has changed people's lives, the challenges we face today are in keeping with any endeavour that brings far-reaching change. Alhaji, I've said it before, you will come back begging for my Cold Fusion formula, and by that time, I will make you pay even more than..."

He was interrupted as my standard issue SML beeper beeped urgently from my pocket. I reached for it and could see the alarming red glow it emitted even before I placed it to my ear to listen. As the message cycled to the end, its import must have shown on my face. They both looked at me with a mixture of justification, expectation and a slight tinge of dread.

"I'm being recalled to the Red Zone, we have a Code-Red." I explained, activating the speaker on the beeper and replaying the message for their benefit. The automated voice rang out and echoed across the large room with insistence.

"Agent Kamorudeen. This is a Code-Red, I repeat, this is a Code-Red. Our analytics show that you are within a thousand mile radius of the Red Zone, you are requested to report to the Red Zone immediately, I repeat, this is a Code-Red!"

They both stared at me in silence for a few seconds as if they had just heard of someone's death, then the old man shrugged his shoulders and chuckled to himself:

"Agent Kamorudeen...Agent Kamorudeen...kai, you have a cool job sha, no wonder you've refused to join me in business, but as you can see, even in the world of business, we still catch our own fun, we have our own gadgets and we have our own ways..."

"Father, I've got to go..."

"I know, I know....come..."

He led me towards his favourite spot at the centre of the room, reached down to snatch up his iPad and worked at it furiously with one hand.

"Let me have your LIC card."
"Father..."

To say the least, I didn't like the idea. Alhaji Sanni was right behind him.

"He's your father Dami, you might have had your differences but he loves you very much and he wouldn't ask this of you if it wasn't of extreme importance. If he can take this sort of risk with his own child, then you should know what is at stake. It is destiny that has placed you where you are today, as your father's son and as a Red Zone agent."

"But why me? Father, you have a daughter, why not her? I thought she was your favourite, why not ask her? Or she's turned you down? I'm the last resort?"
The old man looked up from his iPad with a frown.

"Dami, the last time I heard from your sister was the last time you both quarrelled in this same room and threw obscene words around like the water market women use in wetting fresh fish on display. At least you honour my call occasionally, she is impenetrable to me."

Alhaji Sanni was almost breathing down my neck now.

"Please Dami, don't waver at this point. We need you to go into this with steely resolve."

I stayed still for almost thirty seconds trying to weigh the implications of what I was about to do. In reality, my mind just crunched through the odds without the rigorous analysis that the act of thinking would suggest because somewhere in my heart, I'd seen the road to take. Alhaji Sanni and the old man might be mad and right off their rockers, but they were mad for the right reasons. I fished out my LIC card and gave it to the old man.

"Thank you Dami."

The words came through Alhaji Sanni's lips with a sigh like he's just had a prayer answered. The old man on the other hand only grunted and barely looked up as he reached out to take the card from me. He pressed some keys on his iPad to log out his own card and then swiped mine along the edge of the device. There were a couple of beeps as the device recognized my card and then transferred the data he had prepared for me to carry.

"Who have you been communicating with on that device since I came in? Is it Ravi Shukhavati or your new girlfriend?"
I wouldn't let him be without goading him. The old man raised an eyebrow in disapproval and grunted a reply as he handed my card back to me.

"Ravi Shukavati's location is known to no one, not even me. That is the way we arranged it."
"You didn't answer my question, I'll take that as a yes, so you had him attend my 'briefing' through a virtual link...I take it he's the one who's prepared the application you've put on my card?"

The old man simply grunted and ignored me as Alhaji guided me towards the door with some words of caution.

"We are not at liberty to discuss Ravi Shukavati beyond what we have revealed to you and the less you know about him the better. Whichever way this whole thing pans out, please do not mention this discussion to anyone, it could put us all in grave danger. The application downloaded to your LIC card is programmed as a chameleon bug. It will clone the personal data on your LIC card and its presence will not be detectable unless there's a special search for it. This will not happen as you cross the different security portals between here and your duty post at the Red Zone till you run the app as we discussed. Please be careful. May Allah grant us success."

As the door slid open before me, the old man called out and I could detect a slight hesitation in his voice.

"Son, we're all depending on you. Please remember, be watchful, do not take anything for granted. Let's have another drink when this is over, no?"

I nodded twice and walked out the door, unable to reply him with comprehensible words. There was nothing else to say, the tremor in his voice had said it all.

6.

COMING HOME

BY
ADEBOLA RAYO

YOU PRESS YOUR FACE AGAINST THE WINDOW and stare, trying to make out the species of the fish as they swim past. When you were younger you used to tell your Mom that the fish were calling to you as the train went by. You remember saying it once when Grandma was on the train with you , you smile now as you recall the look on her face that day; the speed with which her jaw dropped, then the panic as she grabbed your mother's hand and told her, "Eh, Iya Tola, this is erm, erm, how do you people say it in *Oyinbo, erm, abomination, yes this is abomination, fish calling to her? Is she *Ogbanje? They want to take my only granddaughter away eh? *Olounmaje!"

You remember how she would not stop talking and clicking her fingers together till your mom switched seats with you so that she was between you and the window and you could no longer see the offending fishes.

It's been sixteen years since you made this journey, the same number of years since you last saw your father. You wonder how he will look; you know he will not be as tall as you remember because you will no longer be looking at him from eyes in the head of a four-feet-tall-ten-year-old. You shake yourself out of your reverie as the train pulls into the station at Lagos Island. You step out and walk briskly to the bus that will take you to Obalende. As it speeds off you stare out the window at the bridge snaking overhead. You remember the stories your mom told of a time when that bridge -the third mainland bridge- and not the underwater train was the major link between the Mainland and the Island, how it was also scary because sometimes at night, robbers would lay siege on the bridge and even throw people over. Now you smile, still wondering as you did then if it was really true. You cannot think of any robber who would dare attack a car; with the defence mechanisms the robot drivers have, it is more probable that the robber would be chopped up and thrown over as fish food.

You follow the directions blinking on your GPRS wrist band from the bus stop to McCarthy Street. Neon lights flash around you, advertising wares of all kinds, you see one for phone chips and it reminds you that you need to sync yours to a Lagos network. You hesitate briefly then walk on, you are too filled with anxiety to sit still for the five minutes it would take to scan the chip embedded in your palm and sync it.

Years of living in New York haven't taken away that feeling you get when you are surrounded by skyscrapers, now it suffuses you again; you feel as if you are becoming shorter with each step you take. In New York, you had learnt to push it aside but these unfamiliar streets will not let you, so you walk faster, scanning the numbers on the wrought iron gates and when you finally get to 20B your brows furrow. Sixteen years ago, it was the only building that wasn't a skyscraper, it had been a triangle shaped five-storey building painted in blue with the logo of cowbell milk all over it. Your father had refused to let the government acquire it. Your mom told you he had challenged their compulsory acquisition and had been embroiled in a legal battle with them, based on principle, he claimed. "He and his damned principles," she had said at the time. You stare at the

building; it had to have at least forty floors. Guess he won, you think to yourself.

You walk to the front door and scan the labels on the buzzers; you press the buzzer for Martins. As you wait, you think, I should have called him, what if he doesn't want to see me? Then you remember that was exactly why you did not call the phone number your mom gave you, that was why you asked her where he lived and you were glad when she said he was still at the same place. A woman's voice from the speaker asks who you are. You do not tell her; instead you ask if Mr. Martins is in. She asks who you are again, before you can answer you hear his voice in the background, as coarse as you remember, sandpaper on wood you think. He comes on and asks who you are, you say, "Tola." That's all you say; Tola. You wait but all you hear is heavy breathing, yours or his, you cannot quite tell. Then, the click as the door opens.

It's the early hours of the morning, you had not planned to stay over but he insisted, sending home the lady he introduced to you as his girlfriend, she could not be much older than you. You and your father sat up all night talking. You had not imagined that was how it would be. You had imagined a short meeting, two strangers who would have nothing to say to each other but there you both were, sipping cold kunu, swapping stories and frantically closing the gulf that had taken its time over sixteen years to separate you.

You ask him if he doesn't have to work tomorrow and he tells you the next two days are public holidays in celebration of a decade of independence. You tell him how you always dreamt of coming back to Nigeria after you and your mom left. To see him again, you say; to spend holidays with him as you used to and have the cross - country road trips he always planned for you. You tell him how you never imagined there would be no Nigeria to come back to, just Lagos.

He is staring at the can of kunu in front of him; he does not seem to have heard you. "What independence are they celebrating? Ten years of independence from Nigeria, so? Is that reason enough to waste two days of productivity?" You wonder if he is talking to you or to himself, you do not know what to do, what to say, so you take a noisy sip, hoping it would distract him. He does not seem to notice. He tells you you should be glad that you did not come back to Nigeria. You ask him why, ask him how Lagos seceded successfully without any bloodshed as you heard. "Oh, you should have been here," he says. "It was purely comical. You know how Lagos had gradually become a mega-city by the time you and your mom left, or maybe you don't, you were so young. Anyway, the other states and the federal government, they started to get upset, especially in 2048 when Lagos generated more revenue than all the other states and the federal government put together, and you know those Nigerian politicians, unhappy to see any real progress, so they tried to sabotage Lagos."

He stares hard at you as though willing you to understand, you nod vigorously and he continues. "First it was constitutional technicalities that caused Lagos not to get enough money to sustain herself even though she generated most of it. The last straw came in 2050, during preparations for the 2051 elections, it was so clear they intended to rig it and install one of their kind as Governor. There were murmurs throughout the state; people were really scared of Lagos going to ruin like the other states." He scratches his head and frowns, his brows touch at the middle just like yours do when you frown. "One morning we woke to hear Governor Alausa announcing secession, and telling everyone who wanted to leave the state to do so within a week. Truth be told I thought it wouldn't last, I thought the Federal Government would declare a war, the kind I had read in history books; the Biafra kind of 1967 and the Niger-Delta kind of 2018 when I was a little boy." He pauses for a while then continues. "And they did, the Federal Government declared a state of emergency and deployed troops to Lagos. It was over within a week though; the moment the Chief of Armed Forces of the Republic of Lagos declared that the state would not hesitate to use her nuclear weapons to fight this war. I tell you Tola, not many of us had imagined Lagos had any such thing. For good measure, they hit two

of Nigeria's largest oil reserves. Some formula the scientists here came up with, they used it to dry up an estimated two million barrels of crude oil in one night. Tola mi, Nigeria gave up without a fight o."

You stare at him in shocked silence, now you understand why it seemed that Lagos had become an independent, developed country over night. Nuclear weapons! Wow! You think.

The kitchen robot snores loudly, making you jump out of your seat. Your father laughs at you; you chide him, asking why he hasn't upgraded to the new models that don't sleep. He tells you how he hates the damn robots. "Getting underfoot all the time, too efficient," he rants. "I can't even have clutter in my life anymore with them around." You remember how scattered his apartment used to be when you were a little girl, how his papers would be strewn on the couch, the floor, the tables, just everywhere. You tell him that and you both have a good laugh, he asks you what good a professor is without his papers, without his clutter. You bite your lips and smile. He says, "The other day, I was lying on the couch, forgetting that I had programmed Kleen for 10am, there I was, lying peacefully one moment, the next I and the couch were suspended mid-air, held up by one of its arms and the bloody robot was whirling away beneath. Scared the shit out of me I tell you. That is what happens when you can no longer hire a good old fashioned cleaning lady. People have become lazy I tell you."

Suddenly, he claps his hand in excitement. "They are executing a politician tomorrow, do you want to go and watch?" You screech; whaaaat? Then splutter. "That's barbaric, this is 2060! Lagos is supposed to be a developed country, how can you still have the death sentence? Even Nigeria has abolished it." He laughs, imitates you, and then he becomes serious. "Why do you think Nigeria is still a third world country...?" Before you can answer he goes on; "...because of her leaders, see eh, in Lagos, the death penalty is only for corrupt public officers, those who have embezzled money or committed some other grave offence against the people of this great country, that...," he raises his voice, slamming a fist on the table, "...Tola mi, that is what keeps this country sane, and safe, otherwise it will be no different from Nigeria. Tomorrow's execution will be the first in three years, and do you know what this pot-bellied idiot did? He stole money that was meant to be used to upgrade the science laboratories in secondary schools of his local government. Does he not deserve to die?" He asks you.

The silence hangs heavy between you two. Your thoughts hop all over the place. Lagos. Nigeria. Your Dad. Your Mom. You pause. You realize he has not once asked about your mom, you remember how she used to say that he had never forgiven her for not marrying him. Now you imagine he probably resents her more for taking you away without telling him. For not letting you have any contact with him after you left. You do not bring it up. You do not want to see a cloud come over him. You do not want to mar the memories of this moment.

Tomorrow you will go to Bar Beach to watch the execution with your father; you tell him it would be good research for your thesis on African Criminal Justice Systems. You do not tell him it's actually because you want to spend a little more time with him before you leave for the Mainland to attend your grandma's burial and then return to New York.

He tells you you will enjoy the outing but that he does not have good clothes because his present girlfriend has awful taste. He tells you he does not want you to be embarrassed, walking with an old, not well dressed man so he brings out his laptop and asks you to help him. He shows you the Eko fashion site, tells you they will deliver the clothes tomorrow if you pick them out now. You upload his picture to the site and place different outfits on him, you are too busy putting women's clothing on him and making him laugh, so that you do not pick out anything he can wear till you fall asleep at the table.

You wake up and take a moment to remember where you are. You see him staring at you. He gets up and leads you to the guest room where you mutter a drowsy goodnight before falling into bed as he smiles and whispers "Tola mi", just as he used to when you were a child. Your last thought as you fall asleep is that you have shrunk to 4ft.

*Oyinbo –English
*Ogbanje –Spirit Child
*Olounmaje –God Forbid

7.

MANGO REPUBLIC

BY

TERH AGBEDEH

IT FEELS LIKE THE CITY'S WATER JUST BROKE. The signs had always been there. The schisms of the first trimester, the upheavals and the unbearable heatwave that heralds downpour. The signs were there.

It was a long time in coming but everyone failed to take note. The scientists who did, who said they were certain, seemed not to have fathomed what they were up against. They may have seen the clouds gather and predicted many times before that there would be rain, but when it did not happen, their anticipation led to a dead end like a spontaneously aborted pregnancy. The threat of rain was an inconvenient sore, which could be hidden under a good dress - a façade of normalcy that could not hide the pus.

The rain this time came with rage akin to vengeance upon those who had taunted it and said it could do no harm; that it would fall for a time, and then fizzle away. It started with a drizzle when the night was asleep and everyone had returned to his or her nest after the day's work.

***

It was sixty years into the third millennium and work still defined Lagosians. In fact, we did more work than ever before, when we stepped out in the morning we were termites whose abode had been crushed. You were either working or you were nothing, worse than an area boy and not to be seen within the city. I know because I experienced it first-hand, I would say I have enjoyed grace because I have wallowed in the grass of area boyness. Lagos no longer had any patience for lazy people and beggars were cast out, banished to the famished ends of the country. The Sahara had encroached way past the Niger and Benue rivers and everyone who could, took the road to sprawling Lagos, a city where dreams took shape and soared.

"How work?" Was the new lingo, the new how far or wetin dey? It was how we greeted each other on the streets. Everything had changed but much still remained the same.

And if your reply was "I never find work", or something remotely close to that, everyone gave you a wide berth like someone with an incurable and contagious disease. It was more than ever before, 'every man for himself'; but if you desired to work there was always something to do with your hands. People still had family ties but there was a new code, though unwritten, it made it clear that no one was there to hold another's hand.

When you had left the institution where you compulsorily had to spend time, you got a plastic card no bigger than a small square. It was the key to your nest, as the twelve-by-twelve feet of space allocated everyone that had passed through the institutions and come out ready, was called. The card was also your train pass, identity card and let you in and out of the city gates. It was also the key to your EV, electric vehicle, if you had earned enough points to own one. Government needed to know where everyone was and how many people were within the enclave at any point in time. This made a census unnecessary and reduced waste to he barest minimum. Everyone got what he or she deserved, what he or she needed.

Even those who were married were entitled to a nest each. The only difference was that they lived next door to each other. When they had kids, and only two were allowed per couple, they got an extra nest. But the buildings on the islands were left the way they were. What Adigun and company did was to reclaim more land from the sea while they decided what to do with the sprawling Lagos Island from CMS to Lekki, all the way down to Epe. Perhaps dredging for the sand for the purpose of reclaiming more land was the only wrong they had committed. They forged ahead despite the public outcry that ensued. They were out to build a model for the best business district in the world but that cursed rain had put a stop to that and turned the clock back many years.

Those who made up the government were picked from the institutions and groomed for that purpose. It was the same for everyone; as soon as you were enrolled you were tested to know what you were born to be, to do. Of course you could take electives from other spheres that fascinated you; the institution encouraged you to know a thing about everything, part of the reason why there was order.

When Aremu Adigun began to lay the foundation for this sort of government there had been an outcry, but thirty years down the road, most people seem to be down with it. More than that, it has added to, rather than taken away from Lagos. It has made the city the envy of other cities all over the world. People have come from far and near to learn how the machinery of Lagos is oiled to make it work so well. That has been a source of revenue because nothing is free, commerce takes precedence over all else. That is why one of the criteria for those who will end up in leadership positions in Lagos is that they must have it in themselves to run businesses.

Adigun had done all the schooling that a man could do in a lifetime and with three PhDs he knew what he was doing when he did what he did.

Nonetheless, the rain truncated this order. Life has always been like that, when you think that all is well, that your barns are full and you can relax and make merry, a major challenge stares you in the face.

***

I have heard it said that it is better to look at things from a distance because a close look reveals all the imperfections. I can say that about pregnancy, about waiting many years to have a baby. I have always loved to attend naming ceremonies and I have never missed an opportunity to join in the drama of it all. When the newborn is presented with honey, salt, palm oil and whatnot, I imagine how it must have been when my parents named me those many years ago. Did I cry or did I laugh? Did I taste what I was given, my introduction to the joys and pains of the world, and spit it out? I imagine how it would be when I am finally able to hold the blood of my blood and bone of my bone in my hands.

It was at the turn of the millennium and I wonder if the celebration was big or small, was a street closed in my name or was it a gathering of close-knit family? Sadly, there is no one to provide me with an answer for I am an orphan and the only heritage from my family is the name, Aromire. I, too, have swum many oceans to get here. I have had many baptisms. This rain was just one of many such rituals.

***

According to Mrs. Aramide Adigun, the administrator of the institution where I ended up, my parents named me after my forebears, who had swam the oceans to birth what has come of age as Lagos.

"Your parents clearly couldn't afford to keep you, they left you outside the gates of the New Heritage Place. Our doors had barely been thrown open and there you were looking like a piece of heaven. At that time I had not completely made up my mind to run the place but I was decided the moment I looked at your face. You looked like you had been handed down to me as a precious gift. I took you with my two hands wide open," the pretty Mrs. Adigun had told me when I summoned the nerve to ask her ten years after I had been at Heritage. I wanted to know everything about the people who gave me life. I wanted to touch someone who had touched them, someone who had an encounter with them, but I came away with empty palms.

"You don't know my parents? You did not get to meet them?" It was hard for me to fathom that, very hard. It hit me like bolts of lightning striking the same place again and again.

"Like I said, they left you outside the gate. I am sorry, but all I have got from them is the note attached to the basket you were placed in. I couldn't help then but to think of how Moses from the Bible had been carried in a similar basket. If they had not named you I'd probably have given you the name Moses," she had said, echoing my thoughts with that note of finality in her voice. It meant that my time was up. I understood, after all, she had so much to do, so many children to take care of with limited resources.

"Thank you," I said. It had been her job to mould me into a little man and her iron hands had taught me well, to be grateful and to be resolute.

"Wait," she said as I dismissed myself. She rummaged through some documents in the shelf behind her and handed me the note my parents had attached to the basket that carried me to the home. It had been written in careful handwriting, very different from mine.

"Thank you," I whispered this time and left. It was the last time I would tell her those words she had taught me, sometimes beating them into me when I showed resistance.

My life remained a question mark with no answers. Had the labour been difficult for my mother? Was she barren for a long time before I came along? Did she suffer miscarriages before I was born bringing her joy, pain? What would have happened if she had kept me rather than leave me at the gates of an orphanage?

It hurt deeply and it was a wound that refused to heal. I

could no longer comprehend the sense of keeping me locked up in an institution because I was an orphan, I bolted. I was only eleven then but I knew exactly what I wanted out of life.

Life at Heritage was not brutish but I knew it had to be short for me. I wanted some measure of autonomy. I didn't want to have people telling me what to do or not to do.

***

I knew the workings of Heritage so it was easy for me to leave without being detected for at least twelve hours. That was all the time I needed. I stole away in one of the trucks that brought supplies to Heritage shortly after dinner, which we ate at 6 p.m. daily.

Huge sections of the city were demolished and rebuilt in phases. The suburbs went first, all the buildings there were demolished and gigantic structures were erected in their place with millions of nests that interconnected and shared the same utilities thereby saving a lot of resources. It was all out construction work like Lagos had never known it since the time of Babatunde Fashola, said to be one of its best administrators. There was a clear-cut plan to keep pollution at bay. Trees and different species of plants were planted in all the spaces in the city.

The structures that housed the nests had farms on the rooftops where crops were cultivated all year round and people who could do the hard work toiled all day long. This was where I found myself.

***

Before farm work on the rooftops, I had lived on the streets as an area boy under Jaja's tutelage. Everyone called him Jaja so I fell in line and did the same.

Jaja's name was like the devil's and it was whispered in government circles as the man who was responsible for all the evil in the land. We had heard of him at Heritage. How he had, with the help of those who trembled at the sound of his voice, waged a war of rebellion against authority. For that he was a wanted man.

I met him my first night out of the orphanage. When he happened upon my resting place in an unfinished structure I thought the devil himself had paid me a visit. He had a huge scar on one side of his face. He roused me with that "dirty slap" Mrs. Adigun always talked about when you got her angry, only she never brought herself to hit me. That would have prepared me for the deafening ringing in my ear and the pain that refused to go away now.

"Smallie, what are you looking for here? You think say free thing dey for Lagos? Carry your dirty body comot for my bed," he screamed at the top of his voice but it seemed to come from a distant void overcome by a dense fog. All his six feet towered over me like an iroko.

Awoken that way I scrambled out of the place half-awake and tumbled as I ran in circles. While I made my futile escape I could hear loud laughter as if from hundreds of mad men. Jaja and his men were laughing at me, at my attempt to escape. Soon many hands were restrained me and I was pinned to the ground as if I were a dangerous animal good only for torture.

"Smallie, who you be and wetin you dey find?" One of them demanded. I was fully awake now, with a throbbing temple.

"You no get voice?" I heard another who made to hit me.

"Leave am. One-blow-seven-die don do am," Jaja's voice boomed again. I only hoped that he was not going to give me another slap.

"So, Smallie, wetin bring you come my kingdom?" Jaja's strong radio voice asked me.

"I want a place to sleep," I said. That elicited laughter from the posse, like rain on a corrugated rooftop. When they stopped laughing there was quiet for what seemed to me like a whole day but was actually a second or two.

"I like this boy," Jaja said and all the king's men who had pinned me on the ground left me alone to find something else to do. Alone with Jaja I paid homage the best way I could.

"Sorry sir," I started.

"Don't worry. If na sleep you wan sleep, you go get am plenty. But no forget, nothing dey free for this Lagos," he told me. I discovered not long after that he meant exactly what he had said. I had moved from the peace of Heritage into the hands of the most notorious hoodlum in the history of Lagos. But it was a move I was not going to regret. Jaja was good for me, he became the father figure that I so wanted to have at that time in my life. He taught me things I could never have learnt had I remained at Heritage. The streets became my playground, my abode. Jaja liked me because I could read; I also tried to teach him how to read and write. I can't say I succeeded in that though. In exchange, he opened the door and allowed me to walk into a new vista that would shape the rest of my life. The things Jaja said to me come back now and again. He said them with careless abandon but those words are like signposts that guide my every move.

"Why you dey always piss?" He'd asked me once.

"I drink a lot of water, water is good for you," I replied. He laughed heartily and said: "But pissing too much no good for you."

Another time, he said: "Life be like buka, you must pay before service."

When I was purging without stop he told me: "Soak Ijebu garri for your purging."

It was not the first time I would be hearing that admonition. I had heeded it in the past but it did not work for me.

"I've tried it before. It did not help me," I told him.

"Try am again, this time make you believe."

I believed and either the condition was tired or it was my conviction, I would never know, but the pain vanished with the ooze.

One day, he asked me how I knew my heart beats in my chest.

"I don't know, I just believe and hope that it is beating," I said. From the smile on his face, it had been a test and I passed well. It was the last time I would be under such scrutiny from Jaja. The look on his face that day stays with me like a father's final gesture to his son.

Whenever I did something right in his estimation, he would tell me to reach out and clean the back of my head. When I did that he would laugh uproariously in that heavy voice of his.

He may have been an outcast and a terror to the government but it was Jaja's influence that got me the job on the farms on the rooftops. Too many people owed him favours. And if that were not the case, he had something he could use against you.

Work on the rooftop farms was hard but you only put in eight hours every day, it didn't matter what day of the week it was. That left me a lot of time to read. I read everything that came my way when I was not doing Jaja's bidding. I, like the many people hanging about Jaja, was a soldier. We did what he told us to do. Being his favourite I spent a lot of time at his feet learning street wisdom. When you merge street wisdom with the type you find at a place like Heritage you are covered for life.

I put in five years with Jaja, then a terrible thing happened. He was found dead in a pool of his own blood on the very streets he had been lord over. No one could say for sure where he had come from but he had made a huge impact in the time that he held sway. No one could fathom who had gunned him down and the case closed even before his blood had dried on the streets he had loved so much.

Perhaps if he did not die when he did, the trajectory of my life would not have taken me to LIST.

The LIST had just been started and the government, which had set it up, was in search of people with a head for books, people who could do scientific research, people who had not been tainted by the various schools of thoughts that were making the rounds.. They found me.

***

I have always known what I wanted. Long before I had my little talk with Mrs. Adigun. Long before the glaciers completely melted at the two coldest points of the earth. Long before the those terrible signs that global warming was real and that green house gasses were responsible started to show. That was long before the city fence came up. Long before the fast trains began to wheeze from one end of the city to the other. Before Aremu Adigun and his cohorts implemented the new master plan for Lagos. Nothing had been left out that would make the city habitable and desirable. There was a dome over our heads to keep the sunrays, which had become truly harsh with age, away. I could never take my eyes away from the wonder that was the subject of conversations all over the world. The dome served a dual purpose; it also tapped solar energy, which was converted to electricity.

Another source of energy was biomass from the sewers that ran the turbines. The sewers were the first project to be carried out in the master plan. Energy was a very important component of the new Lagos so there was research into many more sources, one of which I was actively involved in with my team at the LIST, Lagos Institute of Science and Technology. This research was paramount since all the crude oil reserves in the world had dried up. The whole world was working on alternative fuel research but we were the first to strike real gold. We had come up with a formula that attenuated water so it could not just be used to power cars, trains and other machinery, but it was also used as a healing agent. You soaked yourself in it and all pain was assuaged, disease banished. Except for the new dread, which was very much like cancer and came about from exposure to the sun's rays. Water was also the major source of energy for the nests we dwelt in. Water was originally meant to be life, and with a little creativity this was so. Also, by serendipity, I discovered that zero gravity could be achieved in the nests. This, I also applied to my EV, so that when in gear, it was shrouded in zero gravity the same way electricity flows around the wire rather than through it. Achieve that and increase speed.

But the most challenging of the feats was the dome over our heads. It was a scientific miracle that stretched endlessly, a new sky that kept the harsh rays of the sun at bay protecting the skin from a new kind of deadly cancer that exposure induced.

The substance that made up the dome was synthesised in a laboratory. It was mucus-like and rose like dough in a thin layer that covered a scaffolding-like structure all over the new Lagos. It was a sky within a sky, our protection, which is why the air planes landed outside the city gates.

***

For a long time politicians, plutocrats and pundits believed that water was the future, they swore that ramming it through the membranes of a fuel cell to make electricity was what would power not just cars but all other machinery in the future. And oil majors, who had the money and would go out of business anyway, were willing to bet it on this new technology. I happened to be there right on time to tap into the opportunity. My love affair with water had begun long before I left Heritage. It was a dalliance that would last. While for years it was easy to dismiss water-powered anything as being too energy-intensive to be worthwhile, we, my team and I at LIST, came up with an efficient formula that made financial sense.

The first phase of the project we undertook was the treatment of wastewater. We converted the biogas made from wastewater treatment into electricity. Then we attenuated the water to make it into fuel for the vehicles, which also deployed electricity as backup.

"Science is not magic," I recall my teacher at LIST drumming into me. I have become a believer. Science is not magic and it takes a lot of research and experimentation to come up with results. I had the use of that kind of time at the LIST. It was also here that I met with Rakia. The moment I set my eyes on her I knew that she was the one for me. I cannot tell you how I knew, how I was so certain, but there was no mistake about it.

"Will you marry me?" Those were the very words I spoke to her.

"But you don't know me," she'd said.

"That is true but I intend to know you like the back of my hand, like a part of me. I want you and I to move as if we were one being."

It was a long chase but the day came when Rekia said yes. It gave me a thrill similar to when I first earned my key, it had me covered with goose bumps all over my skin but that was nothing compared to when Rekia moved in next door, after we had gone to the marriage registry and vowed to live as one.

***

Maybe I love naming ceremonies because my wife, Rekia, and I carried a burden, since we met and married twenty-five years ago, we have recorded seven miscarriages. Her womb seems to have been made with eggshells for it shatters too soon, most times as soon as she has weathered the storm of the first trimester, discarding the precious new life. It led me to make a hard decision.

"Having come this far through our challenge, Rekia I'm resigned to my fate. I'd like to have my own child but if that is not possible then I think we should adopt. I don't want to put you through any more pain of carrying a baby and have it end in a miscarriage," I told her. We were floating in zero gravity in my nest. Zero gravity had almost made beds obsolete. When it was time to sleep you pressed a button and your nest lost all gravity.

"Listen to yourself. I'm the one who is going to carry the baby and the doctor has assured me that if I take a break from work for the nine months, there will be no problems. Please let me, if it does not work out then we will do what you want," she pleaded. I was not wired to refuse her anything so I hugged her and kissed her long. Anytime I kissed her, it was like the very first time complete with all the sparks even in zero gravity.

"Is that a yes?" she asked.

"You should know that I could never refuse you anything. And I will be here every step of the way."

It was a hard decision for me but I told myself that what would be would be. If I were to have a child by Rekia then I would have one. I also considered the option of adoption. Things had changed and so had the adoption procedures. Once you showed interest you'd have a child by the end of the day. But though I was an orphan, adoption was not an idea I was completely sold on.

It has not been easy and nothing indicated that it would be different this time. Which is why I am surprised that this night, when the wave that carried the rain these many days had ebbed, Rekia's water broke. On this night when all of Lagos Island that could get out had laid siege on the mainland, my wife chose to begin labour, to bring forth life. Like the rain, her labour was long and painful. Rekia was a strong woman imbued with strength forged through hardship. Her parents, rather than dump her like mine had done, chose to endure untold hardship with her by their side. Lagos may have become a place where dreams come true but this was a long time in coming. The city had come to this pass through painful evolution and the people who lived through it had bitter tales to tell. Rekia's parents give face to such people. Even as the flood wiped away many of the residents, Lagos still had its challenges.

***

The drizzle steadily gained momentum into a rainstorm that refused to abate. The streets that had been polished squeaky clean by the street workers had become soggy and ready to burst. For a long time, as far back as anyone could remember, there was no power outage. It filled Lagosians with a certain nostalgia from back in the days of NEPA. There were no generators since they had died a natural death long ago so everyone reached for the rechargeable lamps that had been stowed away. But even that could not roll back the darkness that was so thick it looked like it night even during the day, because the sun had been locked in battle of supremacy with the clouds and the latter seemed to be winning the war.

Seven days had been the benchmark in the past but this was

different. The rain fell cats, then dogs, and elephants, and then some. It fell until everyone lost count of the number of days, until there was nowhere to set foot outside. When the water that had become a huge pond reached the knees, people started to take note. The doomsday preachers who did not stop plying their trade even for a moment to catch their breath said that the thing they had been sermonising about all their lives had finally come. Rapture would happen at any moment. It was the end of the world, doomsday.

So it seemed when the water went above the knees and continued heading northwards. It was the first time this was happening. Even though no one admitted it, a certain fear had taken over, it was eerie and reminiscent of the days of the Biblical Noah; only that this time, no one had built an ark. Global warming and the havoc its neglect would bring upon the earth had become the new gospel but life went on. Denial was the new religion and everyone practised it with hermit-like dexterity.

No one went to work. Lagosians, particularly those who lived on the islands, whether reclaimed from the ocean or primordial, began an exodus unparalleled by any in the history of the people of the world. They had waited till the very last minute so it was haphazard; people took what they could or left everything, leaving with only the shirts on their backs, in search of dry land. Every one of them would have gladly relocated to the dry north of the country, which had over the years dissolved into the Sahara and had become a prison of some sort where lazy people and criminals were sent. Some people tried to swim out and perished. Most were ferried out with the emergency boats provided by the government of Lagos, which were efficient and helped to save many lives. When all was said and done, a third of the population lay dead in the water. It was close to the disaster that had turned the rest of Nigeria desolate and left half the population dead, except for those who were able to find their way to Lagos. It was not a time anyone wanted to recall or talk about.

Lagos, like a woman with a troubled pregnancy, has had a series of miscarriages in the past but that has not stopped the people who keep trooping to the city gates, built to curtail the inflow that

had become a surge. Those who were already inside needed a pass to come back in if they had been out for whatever reason. That led some to a joke that it was the most beautiful prison ever conceived by man. But this was a good prison, one that had saved many a Nigerian from being fried by the sun when the ozone had died a natural death.

The city was working better than most of its counterparts around the world. It had become an eco-city model for Africa with modern building technology, renewable energy sources and the development of an efficient transport system. Even South Africans, whose technology seemed to have been ahead of any African country's before this millennium beckoned had elected to relocate here. An unbearable heat had enveloped their country and turned many parts of the world uninhabitable. There had been a lot of scientific research spearheaded by the LIST, which had made Lagos a Mecca of innovations and all roads led here. In fact, LIST had then just concluded the prototype for the attenuation of water to be used to power machinery and provide electricity. But the damage had already been done long ago with the first tipper of sand used to reclaim land from the sea.

It has been said that at the time of my birth, twenty-five million was the prediction for the number of people that would be living in Lagos in the present day. They too had been wrong, they had not considered the catastrophe that lay ahead, there was twice that number and the city had expanded far beyond its original borders, many thanks to the encroachment of the desert and the oil wells that had long ago turned empty in the Niger Delta and the rest of the world.

Lagos had soared above the calamities that would have undone other cities, nay, calamities that undid other cities. There were skirmishes among some settler tribes and pipeline explosions that took away countless lives. All that seemed like a bad dream in the night easily forgotten in the morning. There is a cenotaph that marks the spot where a multitude is buried far away from the bomb blast that heralded their fall. That accident is just a memory that comes to mind when one passes near the site unlike the tragedy of the flood, which no one can forget.

But like a pretty single woman, Lagos has always drawn suitors to itself. My ancestors, the Awori, who were the first to come hundreds of years ago, came for the sweetness and like everyone else, left her pregnant with rage.

There was no letting up for the rain this time. It had happened many times before, there would be flash floods but then life would return to normal. Everyone would go about his or her business. But that was not going to be the case this time. The pregnancy had come to term and this child must be born whether it was holding a curse in its right hand and a blessing in its left.

When the rain had finally returned to the initial drizzle, some swore it had been on for forty days, others said sixty and some settled for forever. They had lost what they had been accumulating all their lives.

The rain swelled the oceans that surrounded the islands in Lagos to overflowing. When it could no longer overflow, it became like a stagnant lake with no water going in or coming out locking in the dead bodies and debris. It was juicy, messy like an overripe mango waiting for that nudge to fall to the ground and rot. It was the retribution of the land when well-known laws were not obeyed.

***

I think it is safe for me to lay claim to having the same history with the new Lagos. I was born at the turn of the century and abandoned by my parents. I cannot tell you why they left me behind but whenever I look back I think that I can guess. I was just another mouth to feed at a time when resources had become very scarce and there was no one to lend a hand. I hold no grudge against them and I am convinced that I will take very good care of myself. Perhaps if they had kept me I would not have learnt how to fend for myself. I would probably have been banished to the fringes of the country a criminal or lazy bones to till the hard soil for the food Lagosians would eat. I would not have met Rekia and would definitely not be celebrating my baby boy born

198

to me by my wife. Life can be ironic, Lagos Island is no more and the city is in mourning but I am celebrating the birth of my baby.

8.

METAL FEET

BY

TEMITAYO OLOFINLUA

YOU NEED TO GET TO THE TRAIN STATION. You walk fast. Fast as if the long strides could move quicker than the thoughts rushing through your head like an uncontrollable flood. Faster than the moving cloud of smoke from the many industries around you. You need to escape the blasting noise. You cringe and shrink every time you hear the click-click of metal feet walking close by. You take careful steps as you walk through the bright lights of the staircase that leads to the train station. You cannot wait to get out of Ikeja.

You do not say a word to anyone waiting for the 6pm train. They do not say anything to you too. You like the way they mind their business. The way they let you sink into your own world. Your world that is falling apart, the way you suspect the city will soon fall apart. You try to force your tears back to where they come from. You will not cry! You tell yourself he does not deserve your tears. You tell yourself you will be fine. Safe like the baby in the robot-monitored walker in front of you. No, not like that, you hate those bloody

robots. You sniff. The man sitting beside you raises his head from the phone he had been fiddling with. You place your shawl over your shoulders as if the cool air from the air conditioner is too much, and pull your handkerchief across your nose as if you have a cold. Then, you force an 'it-is-well' smile. He does not smile back. You look at his feet and jaw properly. Chiselled lines of metal. You jump to your feet in panic and change seats, your eyes dart around the floor to make sure there are no metal feet close by.

  6pm. The double-decker train arrives. Everyone moves in a file. You make your way into the train with the use of your pass. You take a window seat; you love window seats. They provide an exit from everything happening within you. They take you through different places at once. Staring out of the window, you can tell the places that are changing and the places that would still change; nothing ever remains the same in Lagos. Hardly have you sat than an old woman in a long adire Kaftan takes the seat beside you. You glance furtively at her shoes... you see flesh disappearing into shoes. You heave a sigh of relief. Her wrinkling hands sneak through the long sleeves that seem to swallow it. She raises her huge eyeglasses to take a peep at you. You notice the ring on her fourth finger. You stare at yours - all you see is the lighter skin that shows a ring used to live there. You place your finger close to your nose, as if to smell the light patch.

  Then the tears start. Gushing waters breaking the walls of a dam. You sniff into the handkerchief. The old lady touches you. Are you well? She asks. You know she can see your tears. You know she knows that you are trying to stop them. She calls you child, says you can tell her what it is, that you can pretend she is your mother. Pieces of a scattered puzzle are floating in your head: your husband, the robot, your discovery, your sadness, your exit. You do not understand it yet. You cannot string the thoughts into words. So you lie. That your mother is ill. Cancer. She raises her glasses from her eyes and peers at you. You are uncomfortable. She seems to be looking into your soul. Then she smiles and that feeling passes.

  The warm couch cannot keep your body still. You tune out

the old woman's sympathetic words. You can feel the rumbling of the train on the rails, it is oddly comforting. It is the reason you always sit on the lower deck of the train. You love it because it is closer to the ground. You love it because as a child you felt that it would be so easy to escape in case the emergency lights in the red box ever went on. This train is one of the newest just brought into the country from China. They cover longer distances than the "Made in Lagos" ones. You are running to Badagry.

Badagry. You were born there some thirty years ago. You schooled there. Ten years ago, you met Abdul-Rahman, your husband there. The old lady reminds you of your mother. Only that your mother never touches quietly. She speaks. Your mother never lets any issue rest; she rouses it. What you would tell her about Abdul-Rahman you do not know. She had told you there was no future in the marriage. Only death. You were twenty. He was forty. She said he was old enough to be your father. He limps. He's short. He's from the corrupt breed you remember her saying. That's what they call children of mixed marriages between Lagosians and settlers like Indians, Lebanese, Chinese and Japanese. There were different kinds: the Yorindians, the Igbonese and the Haujaps. It was the way he spoke Yoruba that attracted you to him. This half Lebanese, half Yoruba guy who spoke better Yoruba than you the so called 'son-of-the-soil'.

You remember the first day you saw him. He was arguing with those at the newspaper stand. Light brown skinned man, straight hair blowing in the wind like a woman's as he limped and shouted as if his voice would make him inches taller than the other man. "The Robots have come to stay. Imagine a world where everything works. A world where you can use your brain for something more useful because the robots do the menials." He said this while pushing back the glasses that were slowly tipping off his nose and staring as though he could see the robots marching in from the future already.

A man in a tweed jacket cuts in. "These things that you call robots, they will lead to unemployment. They will lead to disasters we will not be able to handle. We would have to create a new constitution. We would need new laws. Prof Argumentus, you are wrong on this; there are more disadvantages than advantages." The man peered down at the 'Prof' as he spoke. Every morning afterwards, you stopped to watch them for a few minutes on your way to school.

Nothing happened until the next semester. You were to take an online course in Yoruba language. You had a problem accessing the course online so you visited the university, located on the outskirts of Badagry. To your surprise, there he was, your street professor whom you hadn't imagined was actually a real professor. Professor Argumentus as they called him on the street was your Yoruba 506 lecturer. "Ki ni mo le se fun e?" You remember him saying, short and fast, as if in a hurry. Later, he told you he liked you. You liked him too. You loved the way he would look at you, a sparkle in his eyes, his lower lip slightly bent to the right. The way you both never seemed to agree on anything but your arguments always ended in laughter. That was ten years ago. That was before you married him and moved to Ikeja. That was before Ikeja reclaimed its historical role as the technology hotspot of the state. That was before the Robots.

The young man sitting across you intrudes on your thoughts. You only just realize that he's been on the phone since you entered the train. You listen. "I am the Robot Doctor. What kind of robot do you want? What do you want it for?" He talks as if he expects no response from the person at the end of the phone. "Do you want a gynoid that looks like a woman? A Superbot? An ASIMO? We can give you to spec? We can make it look like you? Think like you. Just imagine days when you do not want to go to work. Yes. Your robot can stand in for you. Do you want to repair your old robot? Okay, I have another incoming call. I will call you back." You shiver at his words as he reaches for his other phone, "Hello, this is the Robot Doctor..."

The old lady shakes her head. She mutters. "That young man is unwell you know?" You do not know. Your Abdul-Rahman was not very different from that young man the last time you saw him. He had started talking to himself, talking to her. You remember how it started on the night the two of you listened to the Governor's broadcast on the LagTube. The newly elected governor said that the government had just signed a contract with a Japanese company to install a robot factory in selected cities. You watched your husband's face brighten as your spirit dampened. You worried about what would happen to human beings. Already you had robots in the house, doing the cleaning, the cooking. You worried that these robots would one day develop a mind of theirs and attack humans. Rahman said you were thinking that way because you were being deliberately obtuse. You should get with the times. Maybe get a personal robot and see they are not beyond man's control. Robots are the future. You remember him say. That was when you told him you didn't need a robot, that you wanted a child. His countenance changed as if someone died. As if his library of books was in ruins. "No Temi, you can't do that. We had an agreement. Only pleasure. No children." He said, pushing your head off his thighs. That was the day he began to change.

That was when he began spending longer hours at his computer. You knew it was not the online classes he had to give. He paid less attention to his looks. You knew it wasn't because he was busy. That was when he started clearing off his table as soon as you entered the room. That was when he answered your greetings only with a groan. That was when he stopped touching you and the compliments stopped. No more "my damsel." Only one- liners. "Yes." "No." "Morning." "Gnait." That was when he started spending all his time in the basement and bringing home strange bits and pieces of metal. One day you came back from your flower shop to meet Zara. You remember taking a look at her and screaming. You remember the way she stared at you coolly, crossed her legs and raised an eyebrow, just like you. Just like you. She looked just like you and acted the same. You remember the myriad thoughts that whizzed through your brain. Did you have a long lost twin? Did your parents have another child they never told you about? You dropped your phone in

shock and it was when you bent to pick it up that you noticed. Metal feet! He would not explain anything to you. He owed you nothing he said. Instead he talked to her. She did everything for him. Prepared his meals. Cleaned his room. You told your mother in a chat that he was acting strange. You were too ashamed to tell her he had spent three months building a robot that looked just like you and now she seemed to have replaced you as his wife. She said it was age. That he would change. She asked you if he was using any drugs. You said no. She said maybe he was having problems in the penile department. She said 'penile' as if shy to call penis. She said he would get over it. But you knew the only thing he would get over was you. You had been replaced by a gynoid robochic. Robots have become your present.

The young-man-on-the-phone reels out louder now. The old lady touches him; motions her hand in mid-air, up and down to show that he should keep his voice low. She turns to you and says: "This breed of children, so ill-mannered they never know when to keep quiet. We all have businesses that we do but is the train the right place to shout it out and disturb others?" You nod as if in agreement. You just want to be left alone with your dark thoughts but she won't stop. She tells you things were sane in her time. She tells you that these corrupt children, they could not talk anywhere, they lived apart from Lagosians, they did not mingle. That, she emphasizes, is how they should have remained. She tells you of how they came to call themselves Lasgidites because they wanted to belong. How they married Lagosians and now it was all a blur. Mongrels! She says vehemently. She tells you that even the Hausas now at Sabo, the Igbos at Alaba were not the original residents of Lagos. She clicks her tongue every now and then as she speaks. That's why Lagos is called a settler town. But we Lagosians know we are sons of the soil. First generation of Isale Eko Chiefs. She says beating her chest, a dimple in her wrinkling cheek. That's the same way Rahman beat his chest, only louder whenever he said that he was an original Lasgidite. You hate the way he crawls into your head. You hate that your hatred is not strong enough to keep him out of your mind.

We. Are. Ten. Minutes. Away. From. Badagry. You hear the automated robot voice from the rear of the train. You want to stand and scream till you drown its voice. You want to shove it out of the moving train and watch to see if it would disintegrate and become naught but wires and crunched metals. No blood. That they will never have, you think with a measure of satisfaction. You hate the way they behave like humans. You are convinced there is something evil about them. Maybe it's in the stony look in their eyes. Maybe it is the metal they have not been able to mask. Maybe it is the calculated way they move. You are sure though that they were sent straight from hell to destroy your life. They have to be cast back to hell. Die by fire, the way your mother, sweaty and marching around the room, cast the demons that spoke through your sleep as a child. Those demons the doctor called malaria. You do not believe in anything again but you want something to clear these things off the streets. Maybe then you would turn around and return to Ikeja. Maybe then Abdul-Rahman would stop talking to that thing. Maybe he would call you his damsel again.

You know that you have reached Badagry. You see the new settlements that the state government just built, CUBES, they are called, built on the outskirts for the poor of the city. You wake the old lady. You tell her the train is in Badagry already. She mumbles something about knowing, something about not sleeping, something about listening to the thoughts in your head. You recoil for a moment but she smiles. You smile back, convincing yourself she was only joking. As you step out of the train, you see the huge TV-billboard-screen, tuned to NN24. You listen to the headlines: Couple Married by a Robot in Ikeja. You see a smiling couple with a robot Priest. Protests in Seven Cities of Lagos Over the Introduction of Robot teachers into the Education System. You see images of people in protest on the huge screen. You see the shields pushing them back from approaching the state house; you stare at the police, wonder if they cannot feel the plight of the majority. Then you stare at their feet. Cold metal.

THE AUTHORS

1. **Afolabi Muheez Ashiru** is a management consultant from 8am - 5pm on weekdays and a creative writer at any other time. He loves writing fiction, He loves animals. He has two self-published books to his credit; 'Curse of the Kings' and 'My People's Past'. His other works can also be found at www.ultrastudios.com.

2. **Okey Egboluche** trained as an optometrist at Abia State University, Uturu, Nigeria and as a freelance journalist at the London School of Journalism. He loves to write and is fascinated by African literature. He has written articles in *Saudi Gazette*, *This Day*, *Nigerian Village Square*, *Nigerian Orient News*, *Leadership*, *Nigerian Tribune* and other publications. His short stories have been published on Author Me, AfricanWriter.com and Authors' Den.
He runs a blog, www.iamontopofmygame.blogspot.com (a.k.a. Game Toppers). He loves garden egg and peanut butter.

3. **Chiagozie Fred Nwonwu** is an editor and freelance writer with a bias for speculative fiction. His articles, essays and book reviews have appeared in *Daily Times*, *The Guardian*, *234Next*, *Nigeria Village Square* among others and his fiction has appeared in *AfricanWriter*, *Sentinel Nigeria*, *Naijastories*, *Storytime* and some international anthologies, notably *AfroSF*, the

first PAN-African Science Fiction anthology. He is awaiting the publication of his collection of short stories and working on his first novel.

4. Kofo Akib was born in Nigeria in 1983. She is a native of Ilorin, Kwara State. She studied English at the University of Ilorin, Kwara State. Currently living in Lagos with her husband and two children, Kofo writes poetry, prose and movie scripts. 'A *Starlit Night*', a Sci-fi short story, is her first published work.

5. Ayodele Arigbabu is a founding partner of Architects' Collaborative, an architectural practice based in Lagos, and also directs the activities of the Dream Arts & Design Agency- a hybrid consultancy with interests in design, art, film and publishing. He is a co-author of *The Three Kobo Book* (Evolution Media, 2004) and also authored *A Fistful of Tales* (DADA books, 2009). Ayo writes for film, theatre and comic books. He won the 2001 Liberty Bank Prize for short stories for his short story- 'You Live to Die Once'. He writes on design and the environment for different magazines and newspapers and also publishes the online design magazine and blog- Design Pages.

6. **Adebola Rayo** is a full time writer and editor. Her works have been published in several newspapers and magazines. She is currently working on her first manuscript.

7. **Terh Agbedeh** is a journalist, who also writes poetry and dabbles in photography. He lives in Lagos.

8. **Temitayo Olofinlua** works in Ibadan, Nigeria as a freelance writer and editor. She is the Creative Director of Wordsmithy Media, a company that brings her passions - writing, editing and public relations - together. Her works have been featured online and in print. Her essays have won awards including the Women Learning Partnership Essay Competition, the CIPE Essay contest in 2010 and the Peter Drucker Challenge, 2012.

Also by DADA books

I am memory
by **Jumoke Verissimo**

"In this her first collection of poems, Jumoke Verissimo, remakes language beyond mere lyricism to uncover the roots of pain and the passion that will heal it. She addresses communal hurt as a personal fate that awaits an assured balm....This poet will travel."

- ODIA OFEIMUN (Poet and critic, author *The Poet Lied*)

Nominated for 2009 Association of Nigerian Authors (ANA) / NDDC

Flora Nwapa Prize for Women Writing

1st Prize winner: Carlos Idzia Ahmad Prize for first book of poetry

at the Abuja Writers' Forum 2009 Literary Contest

&

2nd Prize winner: Anthony Agbo Prize for Poetry

at the Abuja Writers' Forum 2009 Literary Contest

A fistful of tales
by **Ayodele Arigbabu**

"Ayo's muscular, playful language is assured, versatile, and stuffed to the gills with energy and joie-de-vivre...'A Fistful of Tales' is a small collection but it packs a mighty punch. ...Ayodele Arigbabu is a writer to watch.

- LIZ JENSEN (Author, *The Paper Eater*)

`Also by DADA books

The Abyssinian Boy
by Onyeka Nwelue

Winner: T.M. Aluko Prize for First Book of fiction & 2nd Prize, Ibrahim Tahir Prize for fiction at the 2009 Abuja Writers Forum Literary Contest

"The Abyssinian Boy teems with people and issues and sights and smells and conflicts and resolutions, rejects and privileged, losers and victors, black, brown and white. It's a multicoloured story. The Abyssinian Boy is essentially a Nigerian interpretation of a contemporary story of India. The book is filled with perpetual storytelling, a form that's practiced by the British-Indian writer Salman Rushdie and used extensively in Akin Adesokan's Roots in the Sky and Okey Ndibe's Arrows of the Rain. One story being told leads to another shorter story and then this breaks into several stories and we are back to the main narrative, like solo takes in jazz music. The Abyssinian Boy attempts to do for New Delhi, aspects of what Rushdie's Midnight's Children did for Bombay."
- Toyin Akinosho, literary critic & publisher,
Africa Oil and Gas Report

The Land of Kalamandahoo
by Ruby Igwe

School work is boring and home work is annoying, so Tega leads his gang- Umar, Tumi and Chigi on an exciting adventure to The Land of Kalamandahoo, but when Tiboko insists on the normal rule, the gang must seek the help of the flowers in order to escape.

Also by DADA books

The Funeral Did Not End
by **Sylva Nze Ifedigbo**

"Amazing! Brilliant! The claim that the short story is an underdeveloped genre in Africa has finally been laid to rest by Sylva Nze Ifedigbo in this scintillating debut. Ifedigbo is the undisputable master of his landscape and his characters. This is art tout court."

*- **Pius Adesanmi**, winner of the Penguin Prize for African Writing*

Cinical Blues
by **Dami Ajayi**

"Beware of Poets who moonlight as Medical Doctors. It's a terrible mix, there is ample evidence to that effect if you engage Dami Ajayi in conversation. He employs strange metaphors in describing the human anatomy, assumes society can be put in a test-tube and analyzed, and he's a hopeless romantic. Thankfully though, it is a terrible mix that produces a fantastic cocktail of poetry. Dami Ajayi's debut runs the risk of being labelled a classic."

*-**Ayodele Arigbabu**, winner of the 2001 Liberty Bank Prize for Short Stories*